Abigail's Secret Journal

Faith Kidz is an imprint of Cook Communications Ministries
Colorado Springs, Colorado 80918
Cook Communications, Paris, Ontario
Kingsway Communications, Eastbourne, England

First printing, 2004
Printed in the United States of America.
1 2 3 4 5 6 7 8 9 10 Printing/Year 08 07 06 05 04

Cover design: Marks & Whetstone
Cover illustration: Jeff Whitlock
Interior design: YaYe Design

Secret Journals of Bible Time Kids

Volume 1

Abigail's Secret Journal

FaithKidz®

Equipping Kids for Life

An Imprint of Cook Communications Ministries • Colorado Springs, CO

To my parents, who faithfully took me to church and sent me each summer to camp, where I began my own personal journey with God at age ten

Contents

Whispers in the Night

Dear Diary,

In the dim glow of an oil lamp, I saw Mama rub ointment on Papa's blistered hands. They thought we kids were asleep, but I strained to hear their whispers—as I have been doing for weeks. I lay very still so five-year-old Saul would not wake up.

"Eli, this work is killing you," said Mama. "And for what? To build fancy homes for Pharaoh and his officers, and a temple to their false gods!"

Papa leaned his head gently against Mama's and sighed. "We must not give up, Susanna. Remember that Moses is God's chosen one. He will know what to do when the time is right. With God's help, he will deliver us safely out of Egypt."

If God is truly with us as Papa claims, why didn't he appoint a leader for our people long before now? Why didn't he stop the wicked ruler who turned our people into slaves many generations ago? And where was God hiding recently, when the Nile River became undrinkable for seven days? Rumor has it that

Bonnie Bruno

Moses struck the water with his staff. Just one tap and the entire river turned into blood? Ha! I think I would have had to see it to believe it. How could an ordinary stick change the mighty Nile?

I think my gullible older brother has fallen under Moses' spell. For days, our land of Goshen has reeked of rotting fish. We had to dig a tunnel deep into the marshy soil near the river just to find water fit to drink.

"Don't you wish we'd been there when Moses lifted his staff over the river?" he said, shaking his head. "Can you imagine? One quick shake and—ta-da!—the Nile turns into blood! Hundreds of fish dive out of the water only to die on the riverbank." Ben rolled his eyes for emphasis. "Moses is amazing!"

He drives me crazy with such drama. You would think a fifteen year old would not act so naïve. Maybe the fish were just sick, or maybe the muddy banks of the Nile somehow turned the churning water from blue to red. I suppose we will never really know.

This one thing I know for sure, though: When I am fifteen, I am not going to believe everything I hear.

Dear Diary,

Grandmother would have a fit if she could read my mind. I look forward to these times when I curl up on my cozy bed to record my thoughts. Moonlight flickers across the page as I write.

I don't dare say it aloud, but I secretly wonder if Moses is taking lessons from Pharaoh's magicians. Mama agrees with Grandmother. They think my "questioning ways" show a lack of faith. But is it wrong to speak what is really on my heart?

Somehow, I believe God understands all my questions, whether they are spoken or silently simmering in my head.

Someday I hope to become a strong woman like Mama. This morning she awoke early to bid Papa good-bye—again. Doesn't she ever tire of saying good-bye?

 She kissed his raw, swollen knuckles before seeing him off. "Take care of yourself, Eli," Mama whispered. They embraced for a long time.

When Papa turned to kiss my forehead, I wanted to ask what he meant last night about Moses. But his tired eyes convinced me to wait. One day soon the time will be right, and Papa will tell me whatever I need to know. Until then, I will keep my ears perked for more whispers in the night.

Mama and I stood at the edge of the road, our arms locked for warmth. Glimmers of yellow light skipped across our faces as the sun aimed its first rays at Goshen. "See you in a few days," she called after Papa. Then she softly added, "God be with you, my love." We watched until he disappeared around the bend.

Each good-bye is harder than the one before. How I long for the day when Papa can return home for good! No more working his fingers to the bone for wicked taskmasters. What a celebration we will have, when he and Ben can work in our fields of flax and barley and tend our small flocks together. Mama thinks that day may arrive sooner than we expect. I can see why Papa nicknamed her Sunshine. She has a way of thinking on the bright side. Mama is the one who holds the family together while Papa is away. She refuses to give up.

From an early age, I noticed something else that is extra-special about my mother. She talks to God and believes that he hears her. I mean, she really believes. If worry or doubt sneak up on her, she has a simple remedy. She'll sit outside under the night sky until the pure beauty of those glimmering stars takes her breath away. That is what she did tonight.

"Our Creator had a wonderful plan, didn't he, Abigail?" she said. "How can anybody study the heavens and not believe?"

Sometimes it is best to just nod and agree with whatever Mama is saying. It must be nice to know—really know—the God who created the world and everything in it.

Mama says I spend too much time pondering. Papa claims I talk too much. Grandmother tells me that I remind her of Grandfather. Maybe it's my brown eyes or the way I purse my lips when I concentrate. Sometimes I catch her staring at me with a faraway expression. She misses Grandfather so.

We all miss him. After Grandfather died, I thought I would never laugh again, but life eventually returned to normal. I know he would not have wanted me to sit around and mope. If Grandfather were here today, he would have the answers to all my questions.

Tova is my very best friend, but lately I have been worried about her. Whenever I invite her over for a visit, she always comes up with an excuse. Too busy. Too tired. Too far to walk. Whatever happened to the days when we would race to finish our chores and meet halfway between her house and mine? A team of oxen could not have kept us apart. BEST FRIENDS FOR-EVER—that is what we promised each other when we were little girls. I miss those carefree days. I hope she is okay.

I think I will talk Mama into making a date-nut loaf. Tova loves Mama's baking, and it will give me a good excuse to drop by her house today.

Dear Diary,

I have decided to change your name from Diary to Friend. You are here whenever I need to pour out my thoughts. You never interrupt me in the middle of a sentence, and so far, you have kept every secret. So there—it is settled. From this day forward, I will call you Friend.

What would I do without you? My mind is like the Nile River. Sometimes it is packed so full of hopes and dreams, it feels like it will overflow. Other times, my head aches from all the thoughts I've stored away—so many questions and too few answers!

For starters, I would like to ask God how he created the moon. How does it hang up there year after year without tumbling to earth? Why does it take so long for a tree to grow, but weeds show up in our garden overnight? Why am I here at this moment in time, instead of sooner—or later? And why does Egypt's leader get away with treating us Israelites like dirt? Why don't you stop him, God?

Frog Frenzy

Dear Friend,

I do not like frogs. No, wait—that is an understatement. I DETEST frogs! So, what do you think I found sunning itself on my sandal first thing this morning? A slippery green frog with huge bulging eyes! I screamed so loud, the grumpy neighbor next-door flew out of her house in a panic.

I think my outburst embarrassed Mama—until she spied three fat frogs lounging near her precious oven in the courtyard. In a split second, she grabbed a broom and let those hoppers know who was in charge. Nobody messes with my mama's oven! Mama and I had no sooner chased those courtyard frogs away when Saul roared into the house all red-faced and sweaty.

"Look! Look!" he shrieked. He opened the folds of his tunic and out dropped six plump croakers. They hit the floor hopping.

"Wait right there!" he hollered on his way back outside. "I have lots more!"

Dear Friend,

Here is a thought to ponder: I wonder if Moses has been waving that big stick around again. I have never seen so many frogs in one day—strange, if you ask me.

Oh, no-ooo. My five-year-old brother is turning into a frog collector! Next, he'll want to teach them froggy tricks. Can't you just see it, Friend? We'll soon be the proud owners of frogs that sit up, roll over, and sing for their dinner.

Grandmother is threatening to move Saul's bed outside if he brings any more critters inside. Saul just laughs. He knows that she wouldn't harm a hair on his little round head. I secretly think he's her favorite.

Dear Friend,

A chorus of frogs serenaded us to sleep last night. (Surprisingly, I slept better than usual, but I sure won't tell my adventurous little brother.)

I'm almost afraid to walk around here barefooted. Mama was up early this morning, moving about the house, opening windows, and straightening up. Saul had better hope that one of his green slimy friends did not make its bed in Mama's bowl of leaven last night! Without leaven, we won't have bread—at least not the tall, fluffy loaves we love.

Oh! Speaking of bread, Tova was glad to see my date-bread surprise yesterday. I held my breath as I made my way to her door, though, because I wasn't sure if she'd be happy to see me or not.

As it turned out, I picked the perfect time to visit. Tova and her mother were laughing hysterically when I arrived. They had chased a bullfrog around the kitchen and finally trapped him inside a pile of dirty laundry. Saul would have loved the chase.

When I tapped on her door, Tova glanced up. "Well, somebody had better pinch me—HARD!" she cried. "I must be dreaming!"

Tova hugged me so tight, I heard my neck pop. "Where have you been, Abigail?" she cried. "I've been so worried about you!"

"No, the question is where have you been?" I said. "I was almost afraid to visit you."

We nibbled date bread and chattered double-time to catch up. Every so often, we would hear that bullfrog, pleading for his life through layers of soiled garments.

"My father says that Goshen's frogs are nothing compared to what's happening in Rameses," said Tova. "The streets there are piled so deep with croakers, he saw a chariot skidding sideways!" Tova shuddered. "Ugh! Frogs make my skin crawl."

"Relax, Tova," I said. "The worst they can do is slobber on you while you sleep. …" Under my breath, I added, "… or invite all their friends to lay eggs in your sandals."

Dear Friend,

NEWSFLASH! The woman next door is calling Saul a neighborhood pest. Our Saul—famous! She is threatening to swat him with her broom if she catches him near another frog. Ha! She doesn't realize how fast that shaggy-haired kid can run. (I almost hope he challenges her. We could use some excitement around here.)

Here's a poem I wrote in honor of our wild week:

Frog Frenzy
Frogs on my sandals, frogs on my bed.
Frogs playing leapfrog over my head.
Frogs in the courtyard, shiny and slick.
How I wish Moses would lose that big stick!

I read my poem to Grandmother.

"Where's your respect, Abigail?" she snapped. "Moses is our spokesman—God's chosen leader."

"It was just a joke," I said, rolling my eyes. Planting a loud kiss on her cheek, I added, "I got my creativity from Grandfather, y'know."

She just made me peel onions for today's pot of stew.

Grandmother's lentil stew recipe could win a contest. When I told her that, she said, "It must be my secret ingredient." She promises to share her secret with me soon, after I turn thirteen. "It's a family secret, protected by us women."

Dear Friend,

Well, I discovered a new frog fact last night. I awoke with a jolt, as something leapt across my face! A frog *can* do much more than slobber on you while you sleep. (Trust me, the details are not pretty.) For the rest of my life, I am going to sleep with one eye open.

If Moses had shown up at my house today, I think I would have grabbed his stick and whacked a few frogs with it.

I would like to meet Moses sometime. I've never seen him, but I think I have a pretty good idea of what he looks like. I picture him wild-eyed, with tangled hair and a long flowing beard. It is hard to imagine someone who claims to have met God in a burning bush. If ever I claimed something so bizarre, people would call me crazy. Nutso. Around-the-bend-and-over-the-city-wall insane!

I wonder what Moses does for fun—when he's not waving that stick around.

Dear Friend,

Wonder of wonders: I could not find a single frog today except for down near the water where they belong. It looks as if somebody scooped them up and hauled them away while we slept. The croakers left us a smelly reminder of their visit, though—a disgusting stench scattered by a strong south wind.

Stiff, dead frogs lie in heaps along the road—victims of over-zealous sandals or brooms. Neighbors were pitching in to bury them all before the flies found them. I'm surprised Saul wasn't out there organizing a noisy funeral procession.

Mama was on one of her cleaning binges. She was determined to scrub every pot, dish, and utensil in the house—even those too high for frogs to reach. And guess who had to help? Yours truly. Saul is old enough to help, but what did he do? He straightened his bed mat and called that work.

The older Saul gets, the more he wants to follow me around. "I'm booo-red, Abby," he whines.

This morning I ignored him, so he changed his tune. "Where's Ben? I miss Ben!"

"Calm down! Ben is working in the fields today," I said.

Saul rarely accepts a no the first time around. He tries to wear everyone down by asking endless questions. "Will you take me to see Ben?"

"No, it's too far to walk. Besides, I'm helping Mama clean. When you're older, maybe Ben will take you to work with him."

"But I miss him NOW!" he wailed. "I want Ben to come home and plaa-ay with me!"

Was I ever this annoying?

Poor Ben. The last thing he needs is a five-year-old under-foot. It has not been easy, accepting the responsibility for Papa's crops, but he hardly ever complains. None of the Israelite men receive pay for their labor in Rameses, so we desperately need our flax and barley in order to survive while Papa is away. Papa counts on Ben to care for our small flocks of sheep and goats, too. The sheep provide wool for Mama's weaving and meat for our table. And what would we do without our faithful goats that supply us with milk?

Working in the fields still beats having to make bricks for Pharaoh's crew. I like to remind him to not worry—Pharaoh recruits only musclemen. Ben is so skinny, Papa constantly asks if he is eating. (Why do parents sometimes ask such silly questions? Does Papa really think Ben has stopped eating?)

Dear Friend,

Ben met a man whose father is one of the elders of our community. He says that Moses delivered a strong message to Pharaoh: "Let our people go!"

Whaaat? Go WHERE?

Something big is about to happen around here. I can feel it.

I have often daydreamed about lands beyond Goshen. What

kind of houses do people live in there, and what do kids do for fun? Do girls there get to attend classes and learn to read and write? I would not mind visiting other lands, but I sure would not want to live there. Goshen is home. It is where I belong.

Can't Pharaoh just let our fathers return to their farmland here in Goshen? Why all this talk of leaving? And who says we all want to leave, anyway? It isn't fair for Moses to speak for everyone like that. He sure didn't ask *me* what I think! If he had asked, I would have given him an earful.

I doubt I have to worry, though. Pharaoh has sworn he will never let us go. He must think he owns us, like those fine golden goblets in his palace. What will he do if some of us *do* try to leave?

I have heard stories about Pharaoh's gigantic army. His chariots are lightning-fast and number in the thousands. We wouldn't stand a chance if he decided to chase us down.

Do you see what's happening, God? Do you care?

The Neighborhood Buzz

Dear Friend,

The neighborhood is abuzz—not with gossip, but with flying insects.

I awoke before dawn this morning to Saul's yelps. "Ouch! Ouch! OUCH!" he wailed, his voice rising to a higher pitch with each cry. Mama fumbled to light a lamp while I staggered through the darkness to investigate.

The air felt thick—damp and heavy. Buzzing insects zigzagged across the room, diving at my arms and neck.

We are used to battling mosquitoes when the Nile River spills over its banks every spring, but this is ridiculous!

I grabbed Saul's favorite blue cloak and waved it in wide circles. "Shoo! Shoo!"

Saul dove for cover. "Mama, make them go away!"

A few seconds later, I smelled something so awful, it made my eyes water and burn. It seemed to be coming from the pockets of Saul's cloak. I reacted by flinging the cloak across the room where it somersaulted to a stop at the end of Grandmother's bed.

Bonnie Bruno

Big mistake! Something strange and shriveled spilled out of a pocket—the rotted remains of a frog! Grandmother can usually sleep through a thunderstorm, but you should have seen her move when I announced, "IT'S A FROG, A VERY DEAD FROG!"

I made Saul collect the stinking little corpse and toss it in the weeds out back. Mama raced close behind, nagging him to scrub his hands before he came anywhere near breakfast. Then she bundled his smelly cloak into a ball and vowed to string him up by his toes if he ever so much as mentioned the word "frog" around our house again.

I expect to find him hanging by his toes any day now.

After our famous fling-the-frog incident, the rest of my morning seemed almost boring. Mama closed the shutters, and so far I haven't heard any new insects buzz by.

Saul made himself at home upon my lap. "Abigail, I want to sing for you."

He peeked up at me through long, dark lashes. "I made this song up myself. It's called 'Frogs, Frogs, I Love Frogs.'"

It was the longest song in history, bar none. But I had to admit, my little brother did look cute, puffing his cheeks in and out and ribbit-ing at the end of every verse. (Did I mention that there were eight verses?)

I must have inherited my appreciation for music from Grandfather. He knew how to turn an ordinary day into a celebration, just by singing. He would have adored Saul's froggy song.

Mama must have inherited her joyful disposition from Grandfather, too. Whenever I look downcast, she points to her heart and reminds me, "Abigail, nobody can rob you of what's in here—not even Pharaoh, or sourpuss neighbors, or those horrible insects."

It's true. Nobody can steal my song! It's mine and mine alone. I can sing inside my head if I have to!

Now I'm humming Saul's frog song, and I'm hoping the rumors about Moses and Pharaoh are not true.

Dear Friend,

Ahhh … the house is quiet, at last. Saul is asleep!

Sometimes Mama watches me while I play with Saul. "Abigail, you have a special way with children," she says. Grandmother always nods and says she thinks I will make a fine mother some-day.

If those two could crawl inside my head, they wouldn't say such a thing. Little do they know that some days I'd like to gag Saul! There's no end to his chattering. His questions begin first thing every morning and end only when he is convinced I am asleep. I have to fake sleep just to shut him up.

There was a time when Mama and Papa wanted more children. They asked God for another baby, but he must have said no. (I wonder if they quit asking?)

I honestly wouldn't mind if they had another baby—as long as it was a girl. Trust me, Friend, I am NOT ready for another frog-toting brother!

Dear Friend,

I never thought I'd see the day when I would actually enjoy doing laundry. Today Mama and I spent the whole morning scrubbing clothes until every trace of brown dirt was gone. I even went for a spur-of-the-moment swim when I tried to rescue one of Papa's tunics from the swirling waters. I am a strong swimmer, but the river won. Papa's tunic floated and dipped its way downstream until I lost sight of it.

I wish my worries would disappear, too.

I've been wondering: What's with these plagues, anyway? First the river turned to blood, and then frogs invaded our home. Now we're under attack by insects. Not just a few, mind you; it's impossible to talk or laugh or sing without swallowing them!

Papa showed up this evening all sweaty and bug-bitten. Dark circles ring his tired eyes. Mama gasped at the sight of him. "Does that mean you're happy to see me?" he kidded.

Tension filled the room as we ate our evening meal. Papa and Mama glanced at each other every so often, as if exchanging a secret code. I tried making small talk, but nobody paid much attention. Ben caught my eye and winked. He always thinks he can read my mind. Fat chance of that!

After dinner, Papa cleared his throat. "We won't be using lamps tonight," he said. "If we turn off the lights for a couple of nights, maybe we can coax these hungry bugs into leaving."

It's getting dark now, so I have to go.

Dear Friend,

Moses claims that God speaks to him when he pays close attention. God tells him exactly what to say to Pharaoh. "Unfortunately, Pharaoh is not a good listener like Moses," said Papa, "so God has to find another way to get his attention. He sends calamities upon the land, like frogs and these hungry insects."

I wish Pharaoh would wake up and listen so we didn't all have to pay for his stubborn ways!

Our herds are suffering from insect bites, too. I kept a close eye on Saul today. He loves animals—it's one thing we have in common—but he'd smuggle goats inside if I hadn't kept an eye on him.

Dear Friend,

A full moon is shooting sparkly streaks of light into our house tonight. I'm curled up on my cozy bed as I write. I think I could get used to Papa's no-lamp rule. I love writing by moonlight!

Mama has promised to reward me if I can make it a full day without complaining. She thinks my "murmuring" has reached the danger point. I learned the fine art of murmuring from Grandfather whose idea of a good time was to sit in a circle of friends and solve the world's problems in an hour.

That's another reason why I miss him. Grandfather let me speak my mind but never called it disrespectful. Once, when I said that I thought Grandmother was too strict, he threw an arm around my shoulder and drew me close. "I do, too," he said with a laugh, "but she's still the best woman under God's blue sky."

He and I saw eye to eye. We had secret signals, too. A wink meant, "We'll talk later." Raised eyebrows meant, "Uh-oh, looks like trouble!" And a quick gesture toward the creek meant, "I'll race you there!" My grandfather was quick, even in his old age.

I found dead bugs in my bread cake this morning. UGH! Grandmother insisted that I wrap a scarf around my head to ward off insects. I made a sour face. "Forget about looking pretty, Abigaily," she snapped. "Life is not about what you wear."

OH, REALLY? Well, I hope that's true, because I will never, ever wear dark, dreary clothes like Grandmother wears. I don't see why widows replace their favorite colors with black. Grandfather loved colors. He would hate seeing his life's mate look so drab. Every now and then, I tuck a red flower in her hair. I know she likes it, even if she pretends otherwise.

Ben left for work today with a cloth wrapped around his nose and mouth. "Oh look! A mysterious princess!" I teased.

"It's about time you recognized my royal status," he shot back.

I watched my brother saunter past the goat pen, down the grassy trail, and across a field separating our home from surrounding flax and barley fields. Ben seems so much taller lately—almost as tall as Papa. Funny, the three years between us didn't seem so huge when we were younger.

I miss Ben when he has to be away. I almost chased after him today when he left for the fields to say how glad I was to have him for a brother. Instead, I opened my mouth to yell good-bye—and received a mouthful of bugs in return.

Buried Secrets

Dear Friend,

If these plagues continue, maybe Pharaoh will fall to his knees and beg us all to leave Egypt. Wouldn't that be a sight to behold? Moses keeps on asking, but Pharaoh acts like he's hard of hearing. If these horrible plagues don't get his attention, what will?

He claims that his time in the wilderness changed his life, and says he met God there. And he talked to him, too. (WHAAAT? Talk to our Creator? I think not!)

According to Moses, God appeared to him in a burning bush and delivered an important message. Papa and Mama believe him, too. They think God gave special instructions to him that day: Deliver this message to Pharaoh: Release our people from bondage and let us leave Egypt—NOW!

God chose Moses to lead all of us Israelites to a promised land—a fertile land where we can live in freedom and worship the one true God. But here's the thing: Moses keeps trying to convince Pharaoh to let us go. You would think he'd be scared into saying yes! I mean, first the river turned to blood, then those noisy frogs invaded our homes. When disgusting insects showed up, Pharaoh still refused to listen. I would like to have been a mouse in the royal palace when God suddenly drove those insects away. Ha! Here one day, gone the next!

Dear Friend,

I wish I could read Moses' thoughts. He must be losing patience with Pharaoh's high-and-mighty attitude. Mama worries that Pharaoh might strike back at Moses by working our people even harder. I wouldn't put anything past him! I remember when he suddenly denied them the straw they needed for making bricks. (Bricks without straw aren't very strong.) Pharaoh's decision forced them to try and find straw themselves, but here's the catch: While they searched, he still insisted that they produce the same daily quota of bricks as always. He is cruel and heartless, and his taskmasters love their whips.

God, would you please keep your eye on Papa for me?

Dear Friend,

Grandmother awoke with a fever a few days ago and has been coughing ever since. It sneaked up on her like a viper in the grass. Mama made a hot chicken broth, which I have been spooning to Grandmother every couple of hours. She is pale as a sun-bleached branch and is too weak to lift a cup to her mouth. At first, she insisted on feeding herself—until she dropped her spoon and splashed broth everywhere. Now she lets me help, but I have to be quick about it.

I wish Grandfather were here to make sense of this. His faith in

God could fill an entire house. He believed that nothing escapes God's notice, not even a single bird on a treetop. "If God took the time to create and care for the creatures we enjoy, won't he take care of the details of our life, too?" I remember him saying.

Dear Friend,

I wonder if God would appear to me in a burning bush like he did for Moses. What a thrill it would be, to hear his voice! I hope God knows how worried I am about Grandmother.

I want to believe that God provides exactly what we need, but can it be true—really? If that's really true, then why does Papa have to work without pay for a rich, selfish ruler like Pharaoh? Wouldn't a loving God put a stop to such cruel, unfair treatment? Hmmm?

A neighbor overheard this at the market this morning: Moses is going to give Pharaoh an ultimatum—a "Let-us-go-or-else!" He's returning to the palace in Rameses today. I feel trouble brewing!

I hope he takes his brother Aaron with him to the meeting. I've heard that whenever Moses gets nervous, he trips over his words. That's okay; God knows his strengths as well as his weaknesses. That's why he appointed Aaron to be his helper.

NEWSFLASH! Our insects are gone! We're scabby and crabby, but I think we've survived. It'll be nice to sleep without insects skidding in for a landing on my nose.

Dear Friend,

One of these days, Pharaoh is going to toss Moses into a deep pit if he's not careful. And if Moses speaks for everyone here in the land of Goshen, we could all end up piled in the pit with him. (Gulp!) My stomach flip-flops just thinking about it.

Bonnie Bruno

Time to go to sleep! Maybe I'll wake up and find out this was all a bad dream.

Dear Friend,

Life keeps changing, and I can hardly keep up. First, the good news: Grandmother slowly but surely regained her strength. She awoke this morning and asked for mush. I figured, anyone who wants mush at dawn must be feeling better! I can't stomach the stuff at dawn or any time!

It's nice to have her up and around again, but as Papa likes to remind us, every celebration arrives with a price. Grandmother is shouting orders again. She's organized and I'm not. She hurries, but I like to take my time.

Dear Friend,

I'm lying in bed, thinking about Creation. It's something I like to do when I can't sleep.

I keep thinking, God made everything on purpose. Everything! I wonder what it might have been like, the moment right before Creation began. It is impossible to figure, and my mind ends up in knots, as usual.

My stomach is in knots tonight, too. I'm upset about something, and I might as well say it: Grandmother didn't even thank me for saving her life! I sat at her bedside for weeks, spooning broth and swabbing her forehead with cool, damp cloths. You would think she'd thank *Somebody!* Instead, the first thing out of her mouth was, "Let's get this place cleaned up. It looks like a wind blew in."

I complained to Mama, but she wasn't very sympathetic. "Get over it, Abby. Grandmother was so ill, she might not remember anything that happened during that time. She loves you and that's what counts."

Maybe. But it would still be nice to hear a simple thank-you.

Well, I survived Grandmother's housecleaning project. We finished not a minute too soon, either. Townsfolk are dashing about, preparing for a huge, black cloud that was seen heading our way—not a storm cloud, but a cloud of FLIES! Everyone is racing to close shutters and seal their doors.

We're huddled inside, waiting. After that horde of insects, a few flies aren't going to hurt us. Ask me if I'm worried.

A passerby called out to Mama just now. "Have you heard, Susanna? Citizens in Rameses are wretching in the streets. Filthy flies have invaded their homes in such thick formations, they've even flown into their babies' nostrils and mouths!"

It makes my stomach roll. I think I'm going to be sick. Thanks to Grandfather's great curiosity about nature, I know what happens when a fly lands on food. YECH! I shared that little piece of information with Saul, who tattled to Mama. "Abigail!" she scolded. "You're upsetting your brother!"

I've been trying to imagine what Pharaoh's palace must look like about now. His servants are probably running around, trying to shoo flies away from those fancy golden platters. We don't own any golden platters—or golden anything, for that matter. But we do plan to eat dinner, and hopefully we'll beat those filthy flies to our food.

Dear Friend,

Here I am, lying on my bed in a plain little house. I glance around the dim room and don't see anything that I would call fancy. I wonder, why are some people born into wealth while others live ordinary lives? Did God know exactly where each of us would end up and what we would become? Did he know my name before I drew my first breath?

When I was very young, I remember asking Grandfather, "How old is God?" He answered with a long, low chuckle and assured me that God was there long before time began.

God is an always—a sure thing then, now, and forever. He's the same Creator who hung the moon that shone on the night I was born. That same moon is casting its warm yellow glow across my room tonight.

Always. I like the sound of that.

Dear Friend,

I can't begin to describe these last couple of days. We waited indoors like prisoners, expecting the worst but praying for God's protection. Hours crept so slowly, I thought a week had passed. I was afraid we would all mold, so every now and then, I'd ease the door open ever so carefully to peek at the sky. And every time, I saw no sign of flies anywhere.

We passed the time by playing a memory game I invented. We sang songs. Grandmother told stories about the "good old days" when she and Grandfather first met. Mama smeared almond butter on wedges of bread and kept our glasses filled with sweet cider. And let's not forget the 1,328 games of hide-and-seek I played with Saul.

Something very odd happened. The swarm of flies never landed in Goshen. It is a mystery known only to God.

One by one, families threw open their doors and poured into the streets, shouting "Hallelujah! God be praised!"

God has smiled upon Goshen today.

Dear Friend,

God has finally lifted the plague of flies from Rameses. He has given Pharaoh another chance to heed the warning of his messenger Moses. I'm sorry to report that Pharaoh has refused to listen—again. He has chosen to risk another round of God's wrath. Sigh. (There is something seriously wrong with that man!)

This time, God has sent boils—painful, oozing sores.

It doesn't matter whether a person lives in the royal palace or in a humble cottage. Every Egyptian, young and old, rich and poor found themselves dotted from head to toe with open sores. I can't help but feel sorry for them. Egyptian families are suffering because of their cold-hearted leader. It doesn't seem fair!

Dear Friend,

I can't figure out how God kept all those flies away from us here in Goshen! And why did he choose to spare every Israelite from the agony of boils? Word spread among Papa's work crew that Pharaoh's entire household is writhing in pain.

If I were Pharaoh, I would tell Moses, "ENOUGH! Pack up and get out, you crazy Israelites! I don't want to see you or your people ever again. Just go!"

Can't you change Pharaoh's heart and make him listen, God?

Dear Friend,

A family who lives on the edge of Goshen reported an unusual event today. They were working in their garden and noticed a sudden drop in temperature. Dark purplish clouds swirled nearby, casting huge, eerie shadows across the land. Within moments, a strong wind picked up and blew the clouds north. There they spread across Egypt like a gigantic blanket.

Here in Goshen, our skies remained cobalt blue.

Papa arrived home with an amazing story. "I had to take refuge from balls of ice the size of my fist!" he said, showing us his hand. "The hail pummeled everything in its path—everything but us Israelites, fleeing for Goshen." While hail beat upon the land of Egypt, Papa's road home was dry. "Surely God is with us!" he declared.

Dear Friend,

It has been nice having Papa home today, but he has to return to Egypt soon. I'm sickened by the thought of saying good-bye again.

Mama prepared Papa's favorite meal—lentil stew with carrots and leeks. It was his mother's recipe, and Mama memorized it before she and Papa wed. "I wouldn't give my heart to your mother until she made this stew," jokes Papa.

Yesterday on his way home from the barley field, Ben and his friend Caleb met a family who was fleeing Egypt. The father told them about a huge thunderstorm that spread quickly across the land. "Hail beat our crops to a pulp! I've never seen such ferocious thunder and lightning! It could not have happened at a worse time, either. Our barley was almost ready to harvest, and our entire crop of flax was in full bloom." He shook his head in disbelief, like a man who had witnessed a terrible tragedy. "There's nothing left—the fields are wiped bare!"

Dear Friend,

I'm having trouble falling asleep. (What else is new?) My thoughts keep skipping three steps ahead, as usual. What if hail ruins our crops, like it did near Rameses? It's possible, you know. How would we manage, with Papa slaving away in Egypt, if we had nothing left to harvest?

A small, still voice reminds me about the flies that never arrived and the hail that completely skipped over Goshen. Don't worry. I will be with you now and always.

I don't understand it, but I feel strangely comforted. Would God really speak to someone like me?

Dear Friend,

I took a deep breath today and asked God a question. It seemed like as good a time as any. (I hope he's not mad at me for asking.) Awful stories have been pouring in from the north—stories of a groaning in the land. Food supplies will soon run out, and the fields will not be ready for another harvest for months.

"Do you see what's happening?" I asked God. "People are starving—STARVING! Do you care?"

I waited for an answer, but God was silent. I wish Grandfather were here. I would ask him to speak to God and try to make some sense of this.

Dear Friend,

I feel like doing back flips!

Tova and her mother stopped by for a visit today. Mama excused me from my chores so she and Tova's mother could talk woman-to-woman without us kids around. Tova and I flew out the door before she could change her mind.

We walked to our special spot down by the stream. We claimed it as our secret meeting place way back when we were adventurous seven-year-olds. A huge old tree marks our spot. I wonder how many times we sprawled in its circle of shade. I bet we have exchanged thousands of secrets there, maybe more.

One day, I found an old chipped planter in the courtyard. It was deep and wide—the perfect size for a friendship jar. Tova and I each brought a few of our favorite items to fill the jar with. We used charcoal to sign our names on the inside edge of the rim. To protect everything inside, we plugged the jar with an old rag and sealed it with three layers of scrap fabric, topped by a flat stone we found at the edge of the stream. We tied a thin rope around the jar to hold the stone in place and then buried our friendship jar at the base of the tree.

When we're older, we'll take our children to that place. We'll hold a little ceremony and unearth our friendship jar. Forever friends—that's what Tova and I are. I hope our children will be forever friends, too.

Surprise, Surprise!

Dear Friend,

Tova's father was caught in that awful hailstorm. He dove into a gully and pulled a bush over him for protection. Thank God he was not injured! Tova says he is having trouble sleeping, though. He still hears the moans of men, women, and children crying out for help.

Tova is upset with Moses. "He has no business stirring things up with Pharaoh!" she says. "Who does he think he is—God?"

Hardly! God doesn't need Moses' help—or anyone else's, for that matter. But he likes to use people like Moses who are willing to obey. At least that's what Papa believes. I don't know what to think.

If God really wanted to free our people, couldn't he accomplish it on his own? He hung the moon and stars, and they're still up there. Couldn't he also set us Israelites free? Does he really need Moses to do the job?

Maybe Tova is right. Maybe Moses is nothing but a troublemaker.

Bonnie Bruno

Dear Friend,

Sometimes I feel so full of wonder about my world, I could burst. Like the other night, I lay on the grass and tried to count the stars. When I was little, I loved studying the night sky. Often, I would fall asleep and Papa would have to carry me to bed.

Back in those days, I believed everything without questioning. Why do I have to try to figure everything out now? Why can't I just relax and let God be God?

Grandmother has been scurrying around the house, straightening this and rearranging that. I don't think she has spoken more than twenty words all day. I wonder what's on her mind?

Mama is keeping a watchful eye on her. I asked her why Grandmother is so quiet. "She's having one of her thinking days," whispered Mama.

Dear Friend,

A hot wind blew across Goshen today, slapping everything in its path. Early this morning, I helped Mama spread wet laundry to dry. We draped the clothes over hot rocks where they would dry quickly and planned to return in an hour or two to gather them up.

I glanced outside a few minutes later—a good thing, too! The wind had scooped up one of Papa's tunics and tossed it across the roof of a neighbor's house! Saul clapped and danced in circles. It doesn't take much to excite a five-year-old. "Can I climb the tree and get it, Abigail," he begged. "Pleeeeeease?"

A burst of wind whipped the tunic off the roof and sent it sailing toward a clump of bushes. Saul scrambled after it and, in one broad leap, tackled the tunic to the ground.

Surprise, Surprise!

My gaze shifted toward the barley field where a muddy brown haze hangs overhead. Ben and Caleb are working there today. They're inseparable—closer than brothers. They've been friends all their lives. It looks like they're going to be eating dirt for dessert—poor boys.

Saul thought it was fun trying to locate his missing clothes. When we returned home, we discovered something far more precious missing—Grandmother!

Grandmother was gone! We searched high and low but found no sign of her anywhere. When we left, she had lain down for a nap. "You go ahead, Susanna," she told Mama. "I'll be fine. I'm just a little tired, that's all."

"It's not like Grandmother to wander off, especially in this wind," said Mama. She slipped a warm cloak around her shoulders and wrapped a scarf tightly around her neck and face. "Latch the door and stay inside, hear? Keep an eye on Saul."

I wanted to hang on her ankles like a toddler and beg her to not leave. The wind was rattling dishes and vibrating our walls. What was Grandmother thinking, heading outdoors in this mess?

I hugged Mama hard before she disappeared into the sandy fog.

Dear God, if you're listening, please find Grandmother. Lead Mama to her, and bring them back home soon. Please?

The wind howls louder than ever. Darkness has set in, and Grandmother and Mama are still gone. I feel a gnawing in the pit of my stomach.

Saul and I have played every game we could think of. I've folded clothes and fixed us apple slices and chunks of onion bread. I'm about to climb the walls. What will I do if Mama and Grandmother don't return tonight? Who will I turn to for help? The grump next door doesn't like me, and I don't know the new

Bonnie Bruno

family on the other side. I don't know when I'll see Papa again, and it would be impossible to find him in Rameses, even if I had a way to travel there.

Dear Friend,

Last night was the longest night of my life. I couldn't just sit there! I knew I had to do something. So I ignored Mama's warning and slid the heavy latch sideways on our door. A strong burst of wind slammed the door open, barely missing Saul. "Get back!" I screamed, and pushed him roughly aside.

Saul wailed and carried on like a wounded pup. I didn't have time to console him. A massive wall of sand was blowing down our street and swirling in great circles across our courtyard. Mama's aloe plant had toppled, its pot shattered in a thousand pieces.

"MAMA! WHERE ARE YOU? MAMA!" I cried out. I received only a blast of sand in return. Gritty particles clung to my teeth and stung my cheeks.

"Help me close this door!" I cried, and Saul hurried over in his muscleman pose. Together we pushed with all our might against the wind until I was able to slide the latch shut again.

Saul huddled in the corner, staring wide-eyed at the door. "Did Mama go to see Papa?" he asked.

I didn't want to speak until I could rinse the grit out of my mouth. "Mama will be back soon. She and Grandmother are taking a little walk."

Saul was not easily fooled. I'm sure he noticed my silence; he asked why I was sad. How do you explain to a five-year-old that he may never see his mama and grandmother again?

Surprise, Surprise!

A loud thud interrupted my reply.

Have you ever tried to unlatch a door with four thumbs?

I swung the door open wide and Grandmother practically fell into the house. Saul raced to greet her, but Mama waved him away. We helped Grandmother to a chair where she laid her head on the table and wept.

Mama took me aside to ask if I was okay. "Yes … uhhh … no, not really," I replied. "Mama, I was so worried! What took you so long?"

She measured her reply carefully, in case Grandmother was listening. "Grandmother was just tending to her garden," she said. "She lost track of time, that's all."

Tending to her garden—in a windstorm? It made no sense to me, but I didn't ask questions. At that moment, I was just glad that they'd both returned home safely.

After Saul went to bed, Mama told me the whole story. Grandmother had slipped into one of her melancholy moods and wanted to be left alone for a while. She headed for her tiny garden plot, but decided to walk to a spot near the river where she and Grandfather used to take their evening strolls. The blowing sand made it hard to see, and she lost her way.

Grandmother always tells me to let someone know before I just take off. Maybe it's time she did the same. I don't think I've ever been so worried. I feel much older than twelve tonight.

Dear Friend,

The wind finally eased up and passed over Goshen. Sunshine bathed our home today, and, other than a few downed branches and dust everywhere, you would never know we had such a windstorm.

If our goats could talk, they would tell quite a story. I checked on them this morning, and their pen is one big sand dune!

The muddy brown cloud has moved north, over the land of Rameses. I hope Papa is alright. I will ask God to protect him as he works. Surely he sees where Papa is this very moment, doesn't he?

Grandmother and Mama had a special talk this morning as they swept the courtyard. I asked why they were laughing and carrying on, which made them laugh harder. It reminded me of the days when they used to spin tales while they cooked. Papa and Grandfather would find them howling over a shared secret.

"What's so funny, Nan?" Grandfather would ask, planting a kiss on Grandmother's head.

"Never mind," she'd reply with a wink aimed at Mama. "It's for us women to know and you to wonder."

Dear Friend,

The day turned out okay in spite of three scorched loaves (my fault). Mama couldn't stay too mad at me for daydreaming because she'd been waiting all day to share big news.

SHE IS EXPECTING A BABY! (That explains why she and Grandmother were acting so weird earlier.) Papa hasn't heard the news yet. I can't wait to see his face when she surprises him.

Dear Friend,

Oh, I hope, hope, HOPE Mama has a girl! A girl would even the score around here. I know deep down, Papa would probably rather have another boy, but I told Mama I am going to pray for a sister.

She laughed at me. "Too late for that. What's done is done, Abigail. God already knows this child by name."

Well, I happen to believe that if God can shift the course of a swarm of flies, he can also give me a sister! I will ask him every day and night until the baby is born.

Dear Friend,

Grandmother shook me from a deep sleep right before dawn. "Get up, Abigaily! You won't want to miss this sunrise!"

God must have spent all night painting pastel swirls across Goshen. Huge strokes of pink crisscrossed the horizon, mixed with splatters of crimson and gold. Grandmother and I huddled together under her heavy cloak, ooh-ing and ahh-ing at dawn's spectacular show.

Grandmother's eyes brimmed with tears. "Grandfather would have loved it," I whispered. She agreed by squeezing my hand.

Dear Friend,

First the baby news, and now this: Mama has a hunch that Papa might show up soon!

"How do you know?" I asked.

She just grinned and answered, "I can hope, can't I?" Well, I hope she's right, because I want to be there when Mama shares her big news with Papa.

Every chance I get, I remind God that I need a sister. I hope he is listening. It's exciting to think that he already knows her name. He knows what she looks like and what she will become. Like it or not, Saul is going to be big brother to a baby sister!

Winds of Change

Dear Friend,

Anticipating a baby is not as carefree as you might think. Before I even woke up, a sour smell drifted to my nose. Mama was throwing up again. It's not exactly the sound I like to hear first thing in the morning.

I dampened a cloth and folded it to fit her forehead. "Here, Mama," I said, trying to keep my voice quiet. "I'll fix something to eat if you're hungry."

Her face was clammy and pale. She motioned me away with a weak, "Thank you, Sweetie. I'll be fine."

I rushed outside and gulped huge helpings of air. Is this what I can look forward to someday when I carry a child? I will soon be thirteen. Some girls marry at thirteen! I hope Papa does not have a husband in mind for me yet. I don't want to marry and end up throwing up every morning. How disgusting!

Besides, most of the boys around here don't look like the marrying type. They're loud and rude and smell like goats. Caleb is the only one I can talk to. He has known me nearly forever. But how could I ever marry my brother's best friend?

Bonnie Bruno

Dear Friend,

Talk about timing! Who should show up today but Ben and Caleb? I wish Ben would let me know when he's planning to drag someone home. My hair was a mess, and my fingers smelled like onions and garlic.

I don't think either boy even noticed me. They roared, all tangle-footed into the house, babbling at once. Ben described a scene so strange, it sounded like one of the stories Grandfather used to spin for us kids on dark summer nights.

"I was minding my business, enjoying a quiet moment while the flock nibbled away in the grassy field," Ben said. "A shadow crossed over us and hung there for a few minutes. The older sheep grew restless and baa-ed until the whole herd joined in."

"Can you please just get to the good part?" I interrupted.

Caleb's eyebrows shot up. "Listen! The craziest thing happened next. When the shadow blew over us, it felt like a furnace blast!"

I heard myself stammer, "Well, what happened next?" Caleb fixed his dark eyes on me and continued. "Abigail, you should have seen it. The wind picked up sand and tossed it north, toward Rameses. The air was so dry, the hair on my neck stood up!"

"North?" I gasped. "North—where Papa's working?"

Mama's face tensed. "Abigail, would you check on Saul, please?"

What was there to check on? He was lying on a bed, napping. Eyes closed. Breathing normal. Mouth closed. Ah-hhh, peace and quiet.

I returned with my report, but Mama had dragged Ben and Caleb into another room where they could talk in private. She was

Winds of Change

worried about Papa. I could feel it. I pressed my ear to the door and stood very still.

"God will close up your ears, child, if you continue in your snoopy ways!" barked Grandmother.

I jumped at her voice. Goosebumps raised on my arms. I hate when she sneaks up on me like that!

I tried to explain why I needed to hear Mama's conversation. Grandmother didn't care to hear excuses. "Idle hands are the devil's workshop," she said and handed me a ball of dough. "Here's a present for you. See what you can make of it."

Then she winked.

Grandmother is rigid (hard-nosed, Grandfather used to say), but I know she loves me. And it is true; I am a Snoop with a capital S. So, what else is new? But that's not necessarily bad, is it? Snooping is different than gossiping. As long as I don't gossip about it, what's the harm?

I kneaded the ball of dough until it felt softer and pliable. Using the rolling tool, I coaxed it into a nice big circle. Hmmmmm. Should I make sweet rolls for Ben's lunch tomorrow? I could send a couple for Caleb, too.

Dear Friend,

The house is still, except for Saul's mumbling. He's talking in his sleep again. (I should take notes and tease him about it tomorrow.)

Shhh-hh! Can you keep another secret, Friend? Lately, when Caleb's dark eyes flash, my stomach flips like a fish out of water. He didn't seem to care that I smelled like onion and garlic, either.

Dear Friend,

Papa is home! Thank you, God! Thank you, thank you, thank you!

I tore up the road to meet him and almost spilled the news about the b-a-b-y. Thanks be to God for freezing my tongue just in time. Why does my mouth get ahead of my brain like that?

After exchanging hugs and kisses, we all gathered inside. "Eli, I have good news," said Mama.

I nodded an agreement. "Very good news, Papa!"

Papa's eyes searched ours for clues. I was not about to spoil Mama's surprise, but my heart was thumping so loud, he must have heard it. "And ...?" Papa asked.

Mama looked at us, as if to ask permission to continue.

"Pleeeease, Mama! Just say it, okay?" I moaned.

"We're having a baby!" Saul squealed. "Another baby!"

Papa laughed and cried and broke into song. It was one of the happiest moments we've shared in a long time.

Dear Friend,

I heard Papa and Mama talking in the wee hours again.

"Pharaoh has not budged," Papa said. "He is not taking Moses seriously. God is going to deliver us out of here before long."

I held my breath and strained to hear.

"But, Eli," Mama protested, carefully measuring her words. "How can we possibly leave that quickly? It would take days for me to pack our belongings! And what about the animals? Must we leave them behind?"

"Susanna, we have no choice. Pharaoh has refused to listen.

The time is growing near, and we must be prepared to move when Moses says 'move.'"

I should have listened to Grandmother. For years, she has been cautioning me about eavesdropping. I cannot help it, though. Nobody around here tells me anything. They treat me like an infant.

Sorry, Grandmother. I have no other choice. I simply must know what's going on! I tiptoed over by the fruit bin, where Ben's snoring wouldn't distract me.

My nose tickled. Please, God ... no sneezes!

"Stop worrying, Susanna," I heard Papa say. "God will guide and protect us—all of us." I peeked around the corner to steal a look at my parents. "All of us," Papa repeated, patting Mama's stomach.

Protect us—from what?

THA-WUMP. THA-WUMP. THA-WUMP. My heart was beating hard.

Then the worst possible thing happened.

"Aaa-chooooo!" I sneezed. "Aaa-CHOOOOO!"

Papa grabbed the lamp and headed my way. "Abigail? Are you okay?"

"I ... uh ... was looking for something to eat." I grabbed a piece of bread. "I'm starving!"

WHEW! He fell for it.

"Help yourself, but put the basket back," he said. "We can't have mice raiding our supplies."

Dear Friend,

I wish I weren't such a snoop. Grandmother is right; I have a serious need to know everything. Once I know, it's impossible to erase.

I can't stop thinking about what I heard last night. Papa's words frightened me. I don't know what to expect. Is he planning to help overthrow Pharaoh? How? And what will happen when Pharaoh discovers the plan? He might arrest Papa and lock him up in a moldy jail—or worse! I can hardly bear to write what my heart is feeling.

Dear Friend,

The sun rose this morning, as always.

The sheep nibbled grass, as always.

Mama tidied the house, as always.

And we made bread.

Except … except today we didn't add yeast. I asked Mama if she'd forgotten the leaven. "Won't the bread be flat and hard without it?" I wondered.

"Kind of," she answered, "but no matter. We're making flatbread today. It's chewy. Try it. You might like it."

"But the dough won't rise without leaven, Mama," I protested.

"That's the point, Abigail. The day will come when we won't have time to wait for dough to rise. Today we're testing our recipe, that's all."

"But why?"

"Goodness, child!" growled Grandmother. "You're beginning to sound like your little brother. Questions, questions, questions."

Saul chose that very moment to sail across the room like an attacking bee, but nobody seemed to notice. Normally, Grandmother would have scooped him up and carried him off to the box where he kept his collection of wooden toys—the ones Grandfather made when Papa was a boy. Grandmother loved running her fingers over the sheep, goat, and little brown oxen.

But not today. Today everyone seemed lost in silent anticipation, like a robin preparing to take its first leap off a limb toward flight.

Papa is still home. He says he won't be returning to Rameses—not now or ever. Grandmother is folding, sweeping, and packing clothes in storage bins. Even our cooking pots! Mama keeps reminding her to leave the kneading bowl near the door where we won't forget it.

I can't stand the secrecy around here! I must find Papa and find out what's going on. Whatever the secret, I am old enough to know.

Dear Friend,

Tova whistled from the edge of the field behind our house today. I raced to meet her, expecting to run to the stream and catch up on local gossip.

But there wasn't time for gossip.

"I've come to say good-bye, Abigail," she said, choking back tears. "I have a lot of packing to do, but don't worry, I'll find you when we reach the wilderness," she told me.

Wilderness? What wilderness? Why hasn't anyone told me anything about a wilderness?

"Tova, you have to tell me what's going on!" I hated crying in front of others, but if I have to cry I would rather do it in front of my best friend.

"Don't worry, Abigail, everything's going to be fine," she said. "We'll see each other again, I promise. Besides," she added, "if you stay here, you won't have anyone to talk to. Everyone in Goshen will be leaving sooner or later, you know."

"Leaving? You must be kidding! But when?" My throat tightened, and hard as I tried, I couldn't hold back the tears. "Leaving—to go where?"

"I'm not sure," Tova said. "But you should stop crying, or your face will swell up like a frog!"

Tova and I hugged so hard, it left marks on my arms.

Dear Friend,

It feels like the bottom has fallen out of my world. I need answers, and I need them now! Until then, how can I rest?

Papa and Mama must still think of me as a little girl. But I'm not their little girl anymore. I don't need to be shielded from the truth. I have the right to know what's going on.

I'll bet Ben knows. Maybe I can coax the truth out of him.

Papa Calls a Meeting

Dear Friend,

Tova was right. I cried so hard, I woke up looking like one of the frogs Saul used to haul home.

Today the skies to the north were bleary and dark. We're hearing stories about swarms of hungry locusts that have devoured every stem, leaf, and blade of grass in sight! I remember hearing the hum of insects; I watched them blow in, pushed by the *khamsin*—a hot scorching wind. Strong winds normally blow across the Nile delta this time of year, but nobody remembers ever seeing such a swarm of locusts.

Neighbors here in Goshen poured out of their houses to gawk at the humming cloud. We watched until the swarm passed completely over our territory. How strange that none of them settled here to munch on our balsam and sycamores.

I'm glad the locusts kept on flying, but if I had been born to Egyptian parents, I would feel much differently today.

Dear Friend,

Goshen is hopping with the biggest news ever to hit our valley. It is both exciting and frightful. God has spoken again to Moses and his brother, Aaron. They have passed the message on to our elders, who informed every Israelite family in Goshen.

Papa started to share the news with us after our evening meal. "We will write this day on our hearts and remember it always." Then he stepped outside for a breath of fresh air and didn't return until dusk. The suspense was killing me.

I asked Mama for a hint—just a tiny hint—of Papa's news. I had a feeling it had something to do with the wilderness. Was Tova right?

"Patience, Abigail," said Mama.

After sharing a meal of lentil stew, flatbread, and sweet pudding, Papa gathered us in a tight family circle.

He glanced tenderly at each of us before he began. "Egypt has suffered greatly because of Pharaoh's stubborn heart," he said. "Moses has delivered God's messages, and Pharaoh has repeatedly ignored them. Who could forget the heaps of dead frogs or all those gnats feasting on our arms and legs?"

It's true. Every time Pharaoh turned Moses away, the whole country suffered.

Papa paced. "And who could forget the grace our God imparted to us? He didn't want harm to come to our people, so he set up an invisible wall between them and us. Our mighty God protected us from all the plagues that followed!"

We all nodded our heads.

"Just look around you!" he shouted, opening his arms. "Did any of our crops die? Why, your mother and grandmother have continued weaving garments from flax. Have we lost a single sheep or goat?"

Papa was right. Our crops were spared from the cloud of locusts. Mama and Grandmother had all the flax they needed to weave garments. God spared our cassia trees and balsam bushes. Without balsam, Mama would not have had the soothing ointment to treat Papa's raw, blistered hands.

"And flowers, Papa!" Saul blurted out. "Don't forget the flowers."

Papa laughed. "Of course, my little one," he said, tousling Saul's hair. "Flowers have sprung up everywhere here in Goshen—a sign of the Lord's faithfulness."

I squirmed impatiently in my seat. I couldn't stand the suspense.

"So what's the news, Papa?" I asked.

Grandmother shot me one of her famous narrow-eyed stares. "Abigail, shush! Let your father speak!"

I laid my head on Mama's shoulder, and braced myself.

"I won't try to soften the news," said Papa. "In a few days we will be leaving on a long journey."

I searched Grandmother's eyes for an answer, but she locked her gaze on Papa.

I asked—no, begged—Papa for details. Where are we going? How will we find our way? And most of all—when will we get to return?

Papa sat beside me. I could see he was struggling for the right words.

"Abigail," he said in a near whisper, "please understand, God is about to deliver us from generations of suffering here in Egypt. We will gather as a nation to begin our journey to Canaan—a land our Lord has set aside for us. Never again will we serve the likes of Pharaoh!"

Dear Friend,

I must remember all that happened last night, so I can tell it to my children someday.

After Papa comforted me, he said, "Ten days from now, we will kill and roast a lamb—a firstborn, unspotted male. Before we eat, I will sprinkle the blood of that lamb upon our doorposts. The Lord will pass over every household whose doorpost is marked by the blood of a lamb. Those who obey God's instructions will be spared."

SPARED FROM WHAT! Why was Papa talking in code?

I knew if I waited long enough, Ben would beat me to the question and sure enough, he did. "How is a bloody doorpost going to help us, Papa? I don't get it."

"The firstborn of every family is going to be taken," Papa said quietly. "That includes Pharaoh's own son who would rule someday."

"Is Pharaoh crazy?" I cried. "Doesn't he know that his own son is in danger?"

Papa nodded. "He understands, Abigail. He has known for a long time. His heart is cold and hardened. He refuses to turn from his wicked ways."

My stomach flip-flopped. I thought I was going to be sick. I excused myself and ran outside. I found myself very alone under a starlit sky. Ben soon joined me. We didn't need to talk; he knew exactly how I was feeling. One good thing about having an older brother is that I don't have to explain everything. Ben just knows.

By the time we stepped back inside, Papa had lit the lamps. The meeting was over.

An ominous silence fills our home. Its weight pushes against my shoulders. I wonder if life will ever be the same again.

Good-bye, Goshen

Dear Friend,

I haven't been sleeping very well. Maybe tonight I will. Papa made his way around the room to bless us one by one. Papa is a man of God. I have never seen his faith waver. In fact, the harder Pharaoh worked him, the stronger his faith seemed to grow. Pharaoh's taskmasters could hurt his body, but they never could destroy his faith.

Grandfather would be proud of Papa.

Dear Friend,

Spring has arrived in Goshen. This morning, a lone warbler chirped its chorus of hope. I like to think that it flew all the way from its treetop to entertain me.

These last couple days have felt different. In an odd sort of way, I am relieved to know what lies ahead. No more eavesdropping on mysterious conversations!

The warbler was not the only creature celebrating this day. Mama was singing a praise song, and I realized something else— she is not feeling sick to her stomach anymore. My baby sister is treating her kindly!

I wonder what Tova is thinking. Has she finished packing her belongings? Is she ready to leave? Will I ever get to see my best friend again?

Dear Friend,

Papa heard me talking to Ben about our trip into the wilderness. "It's not a trip, Abigail," he corrected me. "It is a deliverance. God is our deliverer, and Moses is his messenger."

I think Papa feels guilty about making us leave our homeland. If I were a parent, I would surely feel the same.

He must ache inside to have to say good-bye to this beloved land where his ancestors once raised their families. Before Papa was snatched away to build the city of Rameses, he toiled from sunrise to sunset in those fields. I doubt he'll ever find such fertile soil and a rushing stream like this anywhere else.

Grandmother was quieter than usual today. I saw her wince when Papa mentioned Grandfather last night. It won't be easy to leave Grandfather behind. If I had my way, we'd carry his bones with us. He has been gone for a whole year now, but our hearts still ache for him.

Some days I can almost picture the deep wrinkles around Grandfather's eyes. He always called them "smile tracks," but Grandmother called them "age gullies." Those two kept us entertained!

Dear Friend,

I would like to know God the way Mama does. Maybe then I would understand why he chooses lowly creatures like frogs and bugs to get Pharaoh's attention! If I were God, I think I would have sent a stampede of camels or slithering snakes instead. Pharaoh would have hit the road running.

Grandmother thinks I ask too many curious questions. "Some things are for us to wonder and for God to know," she says.

God, do my questions get on your nerves?

Dear Friend,

What to take? What to leave? How will I ever decide?

I've laid out all my favorite belongings and am trying to narrow my choices. Papa says we cannot take everything, but if I smoosh them all together, I might be able to squeeze in more. How can I part with my Tabitha doll, a raggedy cloth friend with big brown eyes and wide friendly smile? Grandmother stitched her for me when I was barely three years old. I named her Tabitha—Tabby for short—because I always hoped for a sister by that name.

Dear Friend,

Our beloved land of Goshen will miss the sound of Mama's laughter and the echo of Ben calling to me across the fields. Will the trees droop their branches in a farewell when we leave? Will the flowers drop their petals as a final tribute? Who will sing and dance and delight in the ever-changing seasons here on the banks of the Nile?

Papa noticed my gloomy expression and invited me to take a little walk with him. We ended up down by the stream. There we lay in the grass at the base of my faithful old oak.

I turned away and willed myself not to cry. I wanted to tell Papa about the friendship jar that Tova and I buried near the tree. I want him to know how special this place had become to me. Instead, I said nothing.

Papa talked and I listened. He makes leaving sound too easy. When I couldn't stand it any longer, I blurted out something that I regretted instantly. I snapped, "Well, if I was grown up with children of my own, I'd be staying! Pharaoh would not chase me off."

Papa cleared his throat. "We are a family, Abigail, a God-fearing family. Pharaoh is not driving us away; God is leading us. We have no choice but to trust and obey."

He wants me to feel excited about our deliverance from Egypt, but I can't! And I won't apologize for how I feel.

During our walk home, Papa leaned across the space between us, took my hand, and squeezed it three times—a silent "I love you." I squeezed four times: "I love you, too."

"Papa," I said, finally breaking the silence, "you say everything will be okay, but how can you know, really?"

He answered in six words: "God has promised to lead us."

After Papa and I returned from our walk, Mama drew me close and whispered, "You're not the only person with feelings, you know. Do you think this tearing away is easy on any of us?"

I can't imagine anyone else feeling as sad as I do this very minute. It feels like we're running away from our problems. Papa always taught us to stand firm and face a problem, so what's his excuse? Why can't we stay and give Pharaoh one more chance to change? Doesn't everyone deserve another chance?

Dear Friend,

I have a million questions as I lie here tonight, but what's the use? How do we know we won't be rounded up and hauled back to Goshen—or worse? I've heard awful stories of what Pharaoh does to people who defy him.

I'm worried about Grandmother, too. Will she be able to keep up with the rest of us? And where will Mama give birth to her baby when the time comes—in a dry, barren wilderness?

Will I ever be able to think about this place without crying? Mama carried me in her belly here in Goshen. When I was born, I breathed Goshen air.

I felt the first blade of grass between my toes here. Everything I know about life I learned in this beautiful Nile delta.

How will I ever be able to call another place home?

If I thought we could return—if this were only a trip—I might feel just a little excited. I wonder if we'll meet wild animals along the way. Papa says he has heard tales of snakes and white leopards that live out in the desert. I hope he's wrong! (I wouldn't mind running into an owl or a lizard, though.)

Where will we sleep? What will we eat? I guess time will tell.

Race to Freedom

Dear Friend,

Wouldn't you know it? Moses has delivered another VIM—Very Important Message. Here's the deal: From now on, our new year will begin this month—March—instead of in September. It'll feel strange to start our calendar in the springtime instead of in the fall. And that's not all. From this day forward, we'll be known as the nation of God—one big happy Israelite family. I'm not so sure about the "happy" part, though. The way I see it, we're going to be one big homeless family soon.

God has issued detailed instructions for every family to follow. The head of each household must choose a lamb from his flock—a healthy firstborn male. The lamb must be as white as the blossoms of a coriander plant—spotless! We'll roast it and consider how God has cared for us during our bondage here in Egypt. It'll also be a time of thanking him for keeping us safe through these months of terrible plagues.

If a family is small (under ten people, like ours), Moses says we must share our lamb with another family or two. Since we number only six, Mama has invited Leah, the grumpy widow woman next door. Her three loud-mouthed children will be coming with her. They're young: aged two, three, and five. Oh, joy.

Papa said to get ready; our deliverance is just around the corner.

Dear Friend,

The biggest, brightest moon is shining on our little home tonight. It's as if God wants to remind me that he's still there. Why is it that when things go well, it's easy to feel his presence? But lately when I start to whisper a prayer, words stick in my throat. I feel nothing and hear nothing.

Silence is an awful thing at a time like this when I need so many answers.

This afternoon Papa and Ben cornered an unsuspecting lamb behind our house. The pathetic little creature was barely a year old, the firstborn lamb of our best ewe. I could not bear to watch the slaughter and shut my eyes so tight, my temples throbbed. (If we had not had company, I would have covered my ears and hummed to drown out the noise.)

When I opened my eyes, the lamb lay dead in a heap at Papa's feet, its blood draining into a basin.

Papa dipped a hyssop branch in the basin and sprinkled blood all around our doorframe. With each shake, he paused to proclaim God's faithfulness.

"God is our protector and our provider. We need not fear the days ahead! He will go before us and lead us safely to our new home. He is worthy of our trust!"

Papa described a Promised Land flowing with milk and honey. "From this day forward, the Egyptians no longer control us!" he shouted. "After 430 years of slavery, we will be known as a new nation of Israelites—the people of a mighty God!"

After Papa sprinkled lamb's blood on our doorposts, he did the same at Leah's house. Her oldest child, an ornery five-year-old, dipped his finger in the blood and chased his sister. I'm glad Mama doesn't usually let Saul play with him. Grandmother looked like she wanted to catch him by the ear and give him a good shake. I volunteered to do it for her.

Once things settled down, Papa's voice grew quiet. "Remember this night always," he said softly, glancing from face to face. "For tonight the Lord will pass over every household. Every firstborn will be killed—both children and animals, except those who followed God's instructions exactly."

I jerked around to look at my older brother. How I hope Papa is right! I don't know what I'd do without Ben.

Ben grinned at me. "Ahhh-hh, Abby," he said, poking my ribs. "I didn't know you cared!"

My cheeks flushed.

The bloody smear on the doorpost was almost dry now. It had faded from a bright red color to a dull streak.

I hope the Lord has very good eyesight.

After sprinkling our doorposts with the lamb's blood, Papa prepared the meat and divided it into quarters. Mama and Leah-the-Grump placed chunks of meat on a long spit over a wood fire. Fat dripped into the flames and sizzled, sending a sweet aroma wafting through the house.

Mama's words are kind and measured; Leah sounds brash in comparison. Mama speaks gently to Saul when he wanders too close to the fire. Leah hollers constantly at her unruly children.

Grandfather used to say that a person could learn much by listening and watching. (So you see, Friend, my eavesdropping does pay off.) It did not take long for me to discover why Leah is cranky.

"Pharaoh thought Daniel should triple the number of bricks he made each day," I heard her tell Mama. Leah shook her head sadly. "My beloved husband died alone, Susanna. Word of his passing didn't reach me for weeks."

Her three children pretended not to hear, but I know better. Their eyes were sad.

I offered to help pat dough into small circles. "Thanks, Sweetie," said Mama, "but we won't be making bread cakes today. We are skipping the leaven, remember?"

"There will be enough so we'll have leftovers for the trip, right?" wondered Saul.

Saul—with the bottomless stomach—always worried about the next meal!

"God will provide everything we need," said Papa, "including food and water."

Saul looked like someone had knocked the wind out of him.

"Better eat up," I whispered.

By the time our meal was ready, I could have easily eaten a camel.

Papa called us together—all ten of us united by our new status as God's nation. He looked funny with his long flowing robe hitched up high into a knot. He instructed us to do the same with ours. "Nothing must hinder us from moving quickly when it is time to go," he explained.

Part of our special meal included bitter herbs like peppermint, dandelion, and horseradish. I didn't see why we had to eat something that stings our tongues, but I followed Papa's lead anyway. "Bitter herbs remind us of the bitter years our fathers and grandfathers spent under Pharaoh's rule," explained Papa.

The endive stung my tongue and lips and made my next bite of roasted lamb taste even sweeter.

"Sweet, like God's deliverance is going to be," said Grandmother.

Dear Friend,

It is in the middle of the night, and everyone is asleep, except me. I woke up thinking about the events of earlier tonight. The night air feels balmy, almost pleasant; so why am I shivering?

We feasted until the only thing left was a platter of bones and a few crumbs of unleavened bread. I helped Mama and Leah clear the table. They chattered away, like two friends preparing for a long-awaited trip. Nobody seems worried about the future, except me. I wonder what Tova is thinking tonight?

I scraped the bones of that little lamb into the garbage, and that's when it hit me: I had eaten my last meal in Goshen!

Dear Friend,

I tossed and turned most of the night. Papa shook me awake long before dawn. His voice sounded urgent. "Abigail, get up! No time to waste!"

Moses had arrived in Goshen with big news. Pharaoh awakened while it was yet dark to discover that his son had been slain in the night. Other families discovered the same thing. All of Egypt was groaning as it grieved the loss of its firstborn children. Even its firstborn animals had died.

Pharaoh called Moses and Aaron to a midnight meeting. Every firstborn of Egypt had died, from Pharaoh's firstborn son right on down to the poorest of the poor. The Lord touched every home—from palaces to dungeons—just as God warned he would.

"You must leave immediately!" roared Pharaoh. "I want you and every last Israelite out of my land NOW!"

Moses reminded Pharaoh of the many years our people slaved in Egypt without pay. "Our purses are empty. How do you expect us to leave immediately?"

Pharaoh granted us riches from our Egyptian neighbors and told Moses to take the goods and get moving.

That's why Papa said, "We have no time to waste!" And that's why he's telling me now to put my writing away and to start packing!

Dear Friend,

It's lunchtime. It feels like it's been three weeks since I've sat down to write.

This morning, Papa and Ben gathered our sheep and goats together.

"What's taking so long?" called Ben.

Saul was holding things up, as usual. "I can't find my shoes!" he whined. Saul would lose his head if it were not attached.

I took pity and found his sandals lying outside in the garden patch.

Grandmother blew out the last oil lamp and tucked it in with our other belongings.

"Time to leave," she whispered.

I breathed deeply to memorize the familiar smell of home. I was glad for darkness, which clung to us like a cloak. Tears flowed freely, and none of us spoke for a long time.

Mama stepped over to offer me a gentle embrace.

"We'll be fine, Sweetie," she said. "We are together, and that's what matters."

Mama placed her precious kneading bowl across my shoulders. "Take care of this for me, Abigail. Guard it with your life, and don't set it down even for a minute."

Every Israelite household has a kneading bowl, but this one is extra-special. Grandfather carved the shallow, rectangular bowl for Mama the year she and Papa married. We use it for mixing and kneading our daily bread dough. I wonder how many loaves of bread sprang from his wooden gift. Grandfather, you are coming with us.

We moved through the streets like mice scurrying across a field. Saul took my hand and held on tight. I tried to make light of the event by entertaining my little brother. "A morning walk is fun, fun, fun!" I sang.

He looked at me like I was crazy. "It's not morning," he said, pointing to the sky. "Can't you see? It's dark."

We fell into step behind Mama, who linked arms with Grand-mother.

"Where's Papa?" asked Saul. "And where's Ben? I want to see Ben!"

"Papa and Ben are right behind us, tending the flocks," I assured him. Saul glanced back every few minutes to be sure we had not lost them.

I spotted the outline of a familiar house. Tova's home looks stripped, forsaken. My heart skipped a beat when I suddenly realized that I might never see my best friend again. "Wait right here," I told Saul and bolted ahead to say my good-bye.

Mama called out to me, but I ignored her plea. I think she sensed that Tova's family had already gone on ahead. Mama was right; the house was empty.

Song of the Heart

Dear Friend,

A huge throng of men, women, and children headed south toward Succoth. All over Goshen, Israelite families traveled to our meeting place where we've set up camp.

I'm sitting in a small patch of shade from a juniper bush. My feet are killing me. I don't think I've ever walked so far in one day, but the shorter route—the coastal highway—would have led us past a string of military forts. Too risky. Papa said we could have been ambushed, or stopped and sent back to Egypt. God directed Moses to turn southeast, toward Succoth, tromping past marshes filled with reeds.

The water looked so cool and inviting. If I had not been saddled with Grandfather's kneading bowl, I might have "accidentally" fallen in. I caught Grandmother staring longingly at the water, too. She threw me an understanding wink. "Don't even think about it, Abigaily," she said with a laugh.

We arrived in Succoth around sundown and pitched our tent at the edge of a small grassy pasture where our flocks could eat their fill.

Saul marched around like he owned the place. "Let's turn rocks over!" he called, waving me over to a pile of stones. Give Saul a pasture and he will entertain himself for hours, chasing insects out of their homes. I lost interest in the creepy-crawly world years ago—except for caterpillars. I love caterpillars.

When we settled down, my stomach registered "empty." I had been packing around the kneading bowl so long, I forgot to take it off! My body protested when Mama helped ease it off my shoulders.

She unwrapped a ball of unleavened dough, saved from last night's feast. We patted the dough into small cakes to bake over the fire. "What's the menu for tonight?" I asked.

My question seemed to startle her. "Bread," she answered matter-of-factly.

"Bread and what else?"

"Just bread, Abigail. What were you expecting, a steaming pot of lamb stew?"

My mind replayed Papa's words, spoken at our last meal together: "God will provide."

"Sorry, Mama. I forgot."

I could tell by Mama's pinched expression that she was hungry, too. While we waited for our bread to bake, I helped Ben scramble up a large rock formation to survey our surroundings. Tents dotted the land like freckles. Papa estimates that we number in the hundreds of thousands.

I scanned the crowd for any sign of kids my age. Tova, where are you? I wonder what my best friend is doing and thinking this very minute. Is she wondering where I am, too?

Dear Friend,

Almost everyone is still asleep. I'm worried about Mama. Last night her ankles were puffy from yesterday's journey. "Lie down, Susanna," Grandmother scolded. "A woman in your delicate condition needs to rest."

Grandmother tied a flap of the tent open to let a soothing breeze whoosh inside. Mama rested on one of the sleeping mats and curled up on her side. Later, I delivered a piece of flatbread to her. "I made it nice and warm, for you and the baby," I said, patting her tummy.

Mama smiled through sleepy eyes. "Thanks, Sweetie. It smells good."

Families milled about, nibbling on bread and talking to one another. Our first night together as a nation erupted into a celebration. In the distance, I heard singing. The song caught on and traveled from site to site, and I surprised myself by clapping along. Never did a meal of flatbread set off such a joyful response.

Some of the men joined arms and danced. Even Papa! I thought, Who is this man? Surely not my *father*!

Dear Friend,

I survived another day of walking.

My mat lies close to the opening of the tent, where light sneaks inside. I'd like to light a lamp, but Papa says we must save our oil for nights without moonlight. For now, God's lamp will have to do.

I think of Papa's dancing last night and can't help but smile. I only wish that I could feel that same kind of joy. Maybe someday I will worry less and feel more at peace with our journey.

I could have choked Saul this morning! He thinks just because he's awake, everyone else should get up, too.

"Pss-sst! Ab'gail!" he whispered, pressing his mouth against my ear. "Look, I see tents everywhere!"

"They're the same tents we saw last night, Saul. Leave me alone. I'm sleeping."

"But look—there's a really big one. I didn't see it last night. Did you see it last night? Huh? That one right over there. Look!" Saul's persistence reminded me to pray again for a baby sister. It will be wonderful to have a sister who doesn't wake me in the mornings with stupid questions.

Sunshine warmed the damp pasture, sending a mist skyward. I closed my eyes and imagined the scene back home in Goshen. I could almost see our morning songbird in its usual spot on the top branch of the cassia tree. How Mama loved that tree, with its spice-producing bark. To the right of the courtyard, in my mind's eye, I could see a tight cluster of anethon bushes welcoming the day. Grandmother and I used to collect anethon leaves, seeds, and stems to dry for cooking. She showed me which parts of the bush could be used for medicine, too.

Grandmother stepped outside and stretched. "Abigail? What are you doing up so early, child?"

"Oh, nothing much. Just thinking, that's all," I told her.

"Trouble sleeping?" she guessed.

"Not at all," I said. "In fact, I was sleeping just fine until ornery Saul woke me up."

"Well, I laid there until the wee hours last night, thinking about your grandfather," she said.

"You must miss him terribly, Grandmother. I know I sure do."

"I miss him more than ever this morning," she replied. Grandmother lifted my chin and looked directly into my eyes. "But life goes on, Abigail. God has delivered us safely out of a horrible life—an impossible life—in Egypt. Grandfather would be happy if he could see us now."

As the great assembly woke up, layers of noise were added to the pastures of Succoth. Children were playing tag while their mothers prepared one more round of boring flatbread.

Dear Friend,

Grandmother seems so happy. You'd think she doesn't have any second thoughts about leaving Goshen. Doesn't she miss waking up in the same place where she lived as a young bride? Doesn't her heart ever stretch toward the spot where Grandfather is buried? At the very least, it seems like she'd be missing her garden. Gardening was her passion. Nobody could raise jumbo vegetables like Grandmother.

Did anyone pass by our house in Goshen today? I'll bet they helped themselves to Grandmother's cucumbers and squash. I wonder, did they stop to think about the person who might have tended such a lovely garden?

We've been marching for three days now. Yesterday we turned northward from Succoth and spent the day journeying to Etham, which sits at the edge of the wilderness. The road ends there, at the churning Red Sea.

"Uh-oh," mumbled Ben. "I smell trouble."

Papa shot Ben an annoyed look. "God is directing Moses at every turn. We must follow in faith, Ben."

Restlessness rippled through the crowd. Women huddled in groups, some balancing babies on their hips. They gabbed about life back in Goshen and guessed how long it will take us to reach Canaan. Older children played tag or made imaginary neighborhoods in the dirt with sticks and rocks. Men and older sons tended to the flocks, casting a concerned eye toward the sea, which stands between us the wilderness.

I wonder if God expects us to swim across.

Dear Friend,

How do I begin to describe all that happened today? Words seem inadequate.

For as long as I live, I shall remember the sights, sounds, and smells of this day.

Churning sea!

Howling winds!

Song of the Heart

Hundreds of racing chariots!

Sweat beading like dewdrops on Papa's forehead.

Soldiers shouting! Babies crying!

We stood fearful and trembling at the edge of the great Red Sea. Panic filled our hearts as we spotted an army of Egyptians rumbling after us!

"Moses!" I heard someone shriek. "Have you brought us out here to die? We'd have been better off staying in Egypt and dying there rather than in this watery grave!"

The angel of God moved behind us in a huge pillar of cloud. It stood as a protective wall between us and the land from which we had journeyed.

Moses stilled the crowd and, in a booming voice, declared that God's salvation was near. He lifted up his staff—the same big stick God had directed him to use back in Egypt—and stretched it out over the sea. In one instant, God sent a mighty wind to roll back the water, leaving a dry path right through the middle of the sea! God caused a strong east wind to blow all night, until the entire seabed became dry land. Thousands of feet pounded out a path across the seabed as we raced to safety on the other side.

Suddenly, a wall of chariots rattled the ground, driven by bloodthirsty soldiers determined to stop our band of fleeing Israelites.

"Abigail!" Papa shouted above the deafening roar. "Keep moving!" He cautioned me to not look back, but I could not resist. Sorry, Papa!

What happened next was beyond amazement. After the entire Egyptian army entered the dry seabed, just as the last Israelite stepped out of the sea, Pharaoh's mighty chariots bogged down in the mud. Wheels loosened and spun off in all directions. The army's frantic chase turned to confusion.

God instructed Moses to stretch his hand out over the sea. Immediately, the water rolled inward and formed high, foamy walls

Bonnie Bruno

before closing in on the Egyptian army. Chariots tumbled and crashed as the angry sea swallowed them up in one big gulp.

My knees were shaking so bad, I had to sit down. Mama and Grandmother hugged each other and cried tears of relief. Families counted heads to make sure everyone had made it safely across.

Not a single person was missing! Moses declared God's deliverance, and you should have heard the ear-splitting cheer!

Dear Friend,

I keep pondering all we've been through in the last day or so. Who but God could have caused the sea to roll back like that?

Friend, I was so afraid! I felt like running away, but where could I go? Surely not back to Goshen. If I turned left or right, the sea would have swallowed me up. We had to keep going.

I can't shake what happened next. If ever there was a miracle, this was it. I am here tonight, able to scribble my thoughts as always, because God delivered us. I don't know how and I don't know why. All I know is that my family is sleeping in peace and security tonight.

Tomorrow we will embark on the most difficult part of our journey. Ahead of us sits a wilderness hugged by mountains. What will we eat and drink? I lick my parched lips and try to remember the last time I enjoyed a long drink of water.

One part of me stands in awe of God's deliverance. The other part secretly wishes that God would change his mind and lead us back where we started. Word of Pharaoh's drowned army surely must have reached Egypt by now. If we were to return, I believe Papa and the other men would be allowed to tend to their flocks and farmlands, instead of slaving away.

Dear Friend,

A song dances inside my head. Mama was humming it again this morning as the pink glow of dawn crept across our camp. I first heard the melody when Moses' sister, Miriam, sang it before the congregation after God led us across the sea. Families joined in and lifted their voices as one. It was the perfect song of thanksgiving.

The melody tiptoed into my dream last night, too. I shudder to think what could have happened had Moses not stepped forward with his staff. Pharaoh's army could have easily run us all down. Or Pharaoh's men could have stopped us short and hauled our fathers back to Egypt right then and there. My heart rejoices that none of us were hurt. Not a hair on our heads was harmed.

We have been following a tall, pillar-shaped formation ever since we entered this wilderness. By day, it looks like a tall cloud, but by night—oh, you should see it! It lights up the encampment with a fiery glow unlike anything I have ever seen.

When the cloud makes a left turn, Moses turns left. When it turns right, Moses turns right. And when it stops, he directs us to set up camp for the night. Moses believes that God sent the cloud as our protection.

Dear Friend,

I think I'll sleep better tonight. Saul felt like talking, so he curled up on my mat for a round of "Guess What?" It did us both good to play a game. Life seemed almost normal today. Not completely, but almost.

After Saul fell asleep, I carried him to his mat and tucked him in. A soft glow fell across his face as he slept. It comes from the tall, flaming pillar—God's presence among us. The pillar casts its light across our entire encampment, like a gigantic hug from God.

Bonnie Bruno

A Deeper Thirst

Dear Friend,

We entered the wilderness of Shur today. A parade of people stretches from here to the horizon.

Younger children straddle the shoulders of their fathers while young men tend to the flocks. Mothers and daughters take turns carrying those precious wooden kneading bowls across slouched shoulders. What would we do if all the kneading bowls disappeared, anyway? Would the sky fall if we had to use an ordinary mixing bowl to make our daily bread?

I told Mama that my shoulders are going to have a kneading bowl-sized dent by the time we reach Canaan.

She answered with a laugh. "We can't make bread without our kneading bowl, Abigail. I promise, you will not have to carry it all the way to Canaan. We'll take turns."

Mama's face is sweaty, her ankles puffy from all the walking. Papa offered to let her ride one of the cows, but she will not hear of it. "I will walk with the others," she said.

I grinned at her insistence. "And Papa thinks I'm the stubborn member of this family?" I joked.

A blast of wind caught up to us, carrying an acrid stench that stung my nostrils. *Yeccch!* It is starting to smell like a stable out here. I have to be careful where I step—if you know what I mean.

Hunger gnaws at my gut night and day. Papa and Mama laid down the law today, though: NO MORE COMPLAINING!

But I'm starving, I tell them. I'm dying of thirst, too. We haven't had a decent drink of water since we left Goshen. My mouth is so dry, it hurts to swallow. I can't speak without my tongue sticking to the roof of my mouth.

"All the more reason to stop complaining," Grandmother says.

The night we roasted the lamb, Papa looked each of us in the eye. He said we must learn to trust more and worry less. So, where's the water? Where's the food? Where is Moses' big stick when we need it?

"Use hunger and thirst wisely, and they will teach you," says Grandmother.

I think Grandmother spent too much time in the sun today.

I pointed to Ben, whose bottom lip now sports an ugly red crack down the middle. He's so thirsty, he has stopped complaining. "What about him?" I ask Grandmother. "How long can he go on like this?"

I would like to corner Moses and ask what he thinks he's doing. He assures us that we will arrive at Marah soon. There we will find water—at last!

I close my eyes and imagine our cool, bubbling stream in Goshen, down the hill near my special tree. I smile at memories, such as the day I dived into the river to rescue Papa's runaway tunic. I would give my right elbow to be able to dangle my toes in the Nile River today.

Moses can take away my home, but he can't erase my memories. Those are mine to keep forever.

Grandmother says I need to leave the past behind me and focus on our future. That's easier said than done, though! Asking me to forget the only place I've ever known is like asking me to forget my name. It's impossible. Goshen will always be home, no matter what.

Writing poetry gives wings to my thoughts. Grandfather used to call my poems "liquid gold." Here's one I made up in my head the other day:

A Question for Moses

Moses, Moses, is it true?
Did God set fire to a bush for you?
And did God say that you're his man
To lead us to the Promised Land?
Moses, Moses, is it true?

Dear Friend,

Ben is turning into the king of bossiness. Today I had a plan and asked if he would help me scout around for water. If we could just locate a stream or pond—anything—we'd be the heroes of the camp. Ben thinks I'm an idiot for suggesting it, and said so.

Well, I'll be thirteen soon, and Ben had better watch out! Once I turn thirteen, I'm not going to put up with his nagging anymore.

Grandmother wagged her bony finger at him. "Tend to your own business and let Abigaily tend to hers!" Good thing Grandmother doesn't know what I was planning or she'd have wagged that finger at me instead of Ben!

Abigaily. I love how she still calls me by that nickname. I was barely four years old when she first used it. I tried to wiggle away while she braided my hair, so she made up a silly "Wiggle-Wormy Abigaily" song. She has been calling me Abigaily ever since.

Grandmother has not assigned a special nickname to Ben or Saul yet. I think she saves her nicknames for VSP (Very Special People)—and girls are VSP. It takes one to know one, and Grandmother is still a girl at heart. I bet she's praying that the new baby is a girl, too.

Dear Friend,

NEWSFLASH! How do you spell shock? Moses led us all the way to Marah, and guess what we found?

Water—lots of it. But did I mention that it isn't fit to drink? That's right! The water tasted so bitter, our herds sniffed at it, but refused to drink.

I didn't say anything because Papa was rubbing his beard, lost in thought. An unwritten rule around here: Never interrupt Papa when he's rubbing his whiskers!

Mama tried to act hopeful, but her vacant stare reflected the truth. She was as worried as I was, not to mention queasy from her "delicate condition," as Grandmother puts it. And speaking of Grandmother, she was quieter than a whisper today.

It didn't take long for the news to spread. After all that trudging toward Marah, we'd found water we couldn't even drink. Angry protests flew from person to person. Despair turned to rage, spreading through the camp like a disease.

I even saw one man shake his fist at God as he cried out, "What do you think you are doing? Do you not care, Lord? Have you led us out here to die in the wilderness?"

"Just wait," Grandmother declared, loud enough for everyone around us to hear. "God isn't done yet."

People threw her dirty looks. Some called her old and crazy, but she persisted. "Just wait and see that the Lord is good."

Saul gripped my hand. The crowd pushed to reach the front where Moses stood in the shadow of the ever-present pillar of cloud.

I strained to see as Moses lifted his face toward the sky. In a booming voice, he passed on all our complaints to God. (Does he think God can't hear us?) He told the Lord how thirsty we are and how we had not had water to drink in three days.

Here's the good part: In a matter of minutes, the pillar of cloud moved. I saw it with my own eyes! It moved until it hovered right above a small, scrubby tree.

God instructed Moses to snap off a branch and toss it into the bitter fountain. He did, and then he cupped his hands and scooped up a drink of water. Moses laughed and called, "Come, drink! God has made the water sweet!"

I gulped water until I thought my sides would burst! It tasted as cool and sweet as the bubbling stream near the old oak in Goshen.

Dear Friend,

I lie here in the middle of the night, listening to the wind rippling the sides of our tent. A soft orangish light glows across our entire encampment. It is the pillar, shining its protection over us. I can't sleep—not from misery, but from pure excitement over all I have witnessed today.

After I drank my fill of sweet water, I thought I'd never know thirst again. Now I find myself thirstier than ever—not for water, Friend, but for more of the God who is able to sweeten even the most bitter undrinkable water. I figure, if God can sweeten a fountain, can't he also heal my homesick heart? Dare I ask the God of Creation for such a favor?

The Reunion

Dear Friend,

After our experience at Marah, Moses delivered a word from the Lord. If we obey the messages his servant Moses tells us, God says he won't send any of the diseases he poured out upon the Egyptians. But if we rebel and turn back to our selfish ways, he won't protect us from hardship.

"Do you really think God would send horrible diseases to us?" I asked Papa. "He loves us too much to punish us like that."

"Abigail, hush! Don't test God!" scolded Papa. "He's a just God and will not be mocked."

I'm not mocking God, and if I could talk to him face to face, I think he'd understand exactly how I feel. Grandfather believed that, too. He used to say that God knew him best—even better than Grandmother did. "And he loves me anyway," he said, "in spite of my warts, moles, and daydreaming ways."

Ah, Grandfather. Where are you when I need you?

Bonnie Bruno

Dear Friend,

Mama found a snake curled up in our kneading bowl today! I thought I was going to die on the spot. Saul and I raced for cover. Mama's scream alerted neighbors, who stopped what they were doing and came running with their staffs ready to whack that serpent silly.

Papa grabbed his own shepherd's staff and hollered, "Stay back, it's a black cobra!" After a flurry of flying sticks, none of us had to worry about that cobra anymore!

Papa poked the snake one more time to make sure it was dead. Then he carried the lifeless serpent to a spot outside the camp. It was the funniest sight—Papa leading the way, followed by Grandmother, who kept reminding him to not touch the creature (as if he would). Saul tagged along behind her, begging, "Pleeeease, Papa, could I have the skin for a belt? Pleeeeease?"

Ben acted like some kind of snake charmer. "You're all such weaklings. 'The Wilderness Weaklings,' that's what this family should be named."

Dear God, please, please, please send me a sister this time!

I would like to see Ben's reaction some night if a black cobra slithered across his sleeping mat! The thought makes me shudder. After that snake scare, I've made an important decision. From now on, I'm going to throw a rock at the kneading bowl before I go near it.

The snake incident left Mama edgy. "There must be a million more just like him," she wailed. "From now on, nobody wanders off alone. Is that understood?"

Papa is taking a more logical approach. He reminded us of three facts:

Snakes are more scared of us than we are of them. (Repeat ten times.)

Snakes prefer nice shady hiding spots, like behind rocks (or in kneading bowls).

Snakes lived in the wilderness long before we came along. We are the intruders, not the other way around.

Dear Friend,

Sometimes I catch Mama staring at the spot where earth brushes sky. Mama, are you homesick like me? I wonder. Do you miss sweet cucumbers from our garden? Can you close your eyes and smell Grandmother's famous basil-lentil stew?

Time drags on here in the wilderness. It was good to drink my fill from the sweet water at Marah, but now I am so hungry, it is all I can think about.

I wish Moses had tried the shorter route. We would have been to Canaan by now—the Promised Land. Maybe we could have sneaked past those army forts along the coast. Who really knows for sure?

Dear Friend,

Mama's morning sickness was gone for a while, but now she feels as queasy as ever. "Morning blahs" she calls it. I offered to share my bread to help settle her lurching stomach, but she wouldn't hear of it. When I reminded her that she is carrying my baby sister, she patted her belly. "Thanks for the reminder," she teased. "I'd almost forgotten." Marah is far behind us now as we journey toward Elim. Moses assures us that we will find water there, but will it be drinkable?

A loud-mouthed neighbor grumbled that we would be better off back in Egypt. "At least we had plenty of food and water there!"

he told anyone who would listen. "Look around you! What does this godforsaken land have to offer? NOTHING!"

Grandmother sized him up and shook her head. "Grumbler and troublemaker, that's what he is. God does not take kindly to grumbling."

At least I keep most of my complaints to myself. I'm so hungry, my growling stomach has become a wilderness lullaby. At night it growls me to sleep, and in the morning, it is there to greet my day.

The longer we journey, the more poetry helps me cope. Poems grow wings and help me soar above my worries. Here's one I wrote and memorized last night.

Questions, Questions

Are you with us, God? Do you hear our cry?
Did you trick us, Lord? Is this all a lie?
Will you turn your back? Will we lose our way?
Was it you who moved the cloud pillar today?

Dear Friend,

I was returning to our camp with an armful of dried branches, when a familiar voice rang out. "Pinch me—quick! I must be dreaming!"

I dropped my bundle of firewood and headed in the direction of the voice. TOVA! She was standing with her back to me, talking to a girl about our age. I sneaked up behind Tova and tackled her with a hug. "Where in the world have you been?"

Tova responded with a polite embrace. She acted like she'd seen me just a few hours ago. "Oh, hi."

I explained how I had stopped at her house to say good-bye, but found it deserted. "I thought I'd never see you again."

The other girl didn't say a word, just stared me down and sized me up. "Well, are you coming or not?" she asked Tova.

"This is Nan," said Tova. "We met in Succoth, and her family has been camping next to us."

Nan looked nice enough, but she sure wasn't big on words. "So, are you homesick for Goshen?" I asked.

Nan flipped a strand of curly hair away from her forehead. "Not really. I could hardly wait to leave. I hated it there."

Tova changed the subject. "So what do you think of Moses and his crazy plan, Abigail?"

"Moses and his crazy plan?" I asked, pretending to not understand. I glanced around to see if anyone was watching or listening. The last thing I needed was for Papa to hear me grumbling about Moses. "It's okay," I lied.

"Yeah, right," laughed Tova. "I can tell you're lying." She rolled her eyes in Nan's direction.

Why was Tova trying to embarrass me?

I shot back with, "Well, it's not like you were looking forward to leaving Goshen, either, Tova. Goshen will always feel like home to me. Someday I want to go back to dig up that you-know-what under our tree down by the stream."

Tova looked like she'd swallowed a fly.

"Dig up what?" laughed Nan. "A body?"

Tova threw me a sharp look. "Oh, Abigail is just homesick, that's all. Nobody in their right mind would want to ever go back to Goshen."

Tova spun on her heels and marched off in the opposite direction, with her new friend trailing close behind. "See you," she called over her shoulder.

"Tova, wait!" I called. "Where will I find you?"

Within seconds, the crowd swallowed them up.

If I could only hush the crowd, I would have scrambled up on a rock and screamed "Tova!" as loud as possible. Maybe she will show up at our next stop—hopefully without Nan so we can really talk this time. I have a lot of questions to ask her, like why she turned into such a brat.

Dear Friend,

Moses sent word through the elders that we will be reaching Elim soon. Elim is known as a lush green oasis for desert travelers. My steps feel lighter as we move toward the twelve springs that await us there.

I am learning to not get my hopes up, though. I mean, look what happened at Marah! The water was so bitter, the animals refused it.

"Moses had better not lose that big stick of his!" I told Papa.

Papa laughed. "Oh, Abigail, don't you know that it isn't about the stick? Moses obeys; that's the important thing. God doesn't need a stick to display his power and might. He just needs a person like Moses, who is willing to trust and obey."

I'm kind of annoyed at Papa tonight. I wish I could tell him how I feel, but he'd probably just frown. He acts like all we have to do is "trust and obey," and everything will be fine.

What about our hunger? What about our thirst? And what about my best friend, who has deserted me for what's-her-name? I'd gladly trust and obey, if I knew for sure that God would help me find Tova again. Without my friend, this journey is going to drag on forever. Are you out there listening, God?

A Light in the Wilderness

Dear Friend,

Grandmother gave me a scare today. She stood up and started swaying. Her face turned ashen and she called out, "Abigail! Help me. I think I'm going to faint!"

Mama and I eased her down onto a shady patch of weeds. "Go find Papa," instructed Mama. "Tell him it's an emergency."

I pushed through the middle of the herd, startling goats and sheep. They scattered in all directions like a raindrop hitting a puddle.

Papa's face flushed with anger. "Abigail! Have you lost your senses?"

"Grandmother almost fainted!" I told him. "Mama sent me to get you."

Papa and I returned with Sassy, a gentle cow that we affectionately named when she was two weeks old. Papa placed a blanket across Sassy's back and helped Grandmother climb up.

Grandmother mumbled a weak protest, which Papa ignored. "Give yourself a break, Mother," he said. "We'll find water soon."

Bonnie Bruno

Papa lifted his eyes heavenward. I knew what he was doing. He talks to God as much as Moses does—maybe more. (I wonder why God chose Moses to lead our people instead of Papa.)

Clumps of bramble bushes dot the landscape as we near Elim. The thud of sandals hitting earth has become our marching tune. Younger children sing songs together as they walk. Older people lean on each other for support or catch an occasional ride on a beast of burden, like Grandmother is doing. And what a burden it is! Our animals look as road-weary as the rest of us.

I hope that Elim delivers what Moses has promised—plenty of water for everyone. I, for one, would like to bathe, but is that asking too much? If I don't bathe soon, I might be mistaken for one of those smelly goats.

Dear Friend,

A healthy pink tint has returned to Grandmother's cheeks. I can tell she's feeling better because today she worried about how she looks to others. She was embarrassed to be riding a cow. I can't say I blame her!

"What kind of a person rides a silly old cow?" she asked.

"A person who almost fainted," I replied.

I patted Sassy on the head and leaned in close. "Sorry, Sassy," I whispered. "Grandmother didn't mean that. You're not silly, and you're certainly not old."

Grandmother managed a laugh—something I haven't heard since we left Goshen. "Come on, Abigaily," she said, offering me her hand. "Help me climb down."

I knew better than to argue. When Grandmother sets her mind to something, she doesn't give up. As soon as her toes touched the ground, she declared, "I had a pretty good view from atop ol' Sassy. In fact, I couldn't help but notice your slumped shoulders, Abigaily. Want to tell me what's wrong?"

I shrugged and mumbled, "Oh, nothing." But Grandmother persisted.

Tears rolled as I described my sour reunion with Tova. "She seems so different, Grandmother. It felt like we hardly knew each other. Then that girl, Nan, snapped her fingers and Tova jumped."

Grandmother kissed the top of my head. (Her clothes smelled hot and dirty like Sassy, but I decided to not mention it.)

"Ah, Abigaily," she said, "God delivered us from a bleak future. He will see us through, and I promise you—someday everything will be made right. Once we settle in Canaan, you and Tova will probably take up right where you left off."

"I hope so," I whispered.

The Promised Land doesn't sound so promising if I lose my best friend during the journey. I've got to find a way to fix our friendship.

Dear Friend,

Wind whips and spins sand in my face with each step of this journey. Our loose footprints disappear in a couple of hours. Will anyone know—or care—that we passed this way?

My heart feels as empty as the house I left behind in Goshen. Never have I trudged for days without a place to call home. Our scenery never changes, except for an occasional bush here and a tree there. And snakes. I have never seen so many snakes in all my life!

On the Move

Sand and rock, rock and sand
Snakes and spiders, sun-baked land
No more garden, no more brook
No more lentil stew to cook
Sand and rock, rock and sand
Lord, how much more can we stand?

Dear Friend,

Papa's voice rang out. "Look—I see palm trees!"

ELIM! I socked the air and hugged sweaty little Saul, who wasn't sure what all the commotion was about. A group of older boys took off running, hoping to drink their fill before the rest of us arrived. I felt like tripping them as they buzzed by. SELFISH CLODS! They kicked up clouds of dust in their race to be first.

"Wait your turn!" hollered a woman balancing a small child on one hip.

"Unruly brats!" yelled another.

"May God help the mother of such selfish boys," tsk-tsked Grandmother. "Whatever happened to courtesy? They should be ashamed!"

The nation of God picked up the pace, like sheep heading toward a watering hole. We were parched and dirty, a people desperately in need of comfort and rest.

The cloud pillar stopped dead center over Elim. A cheer erupted at the front of our assembly as Moses announced that we would set up an encampment here. Elim is a green gift in the middle of a colorless wilderness—a perfect place to sleep away my cares.

Elders among the group handed out instructions. God has provided twelve wells—one for each of our twelve tribes. Excited conversations flew back and forth among friends and strangers alike as we waited for our turn to drink.

How I wanted to slip into the shade of one of those palms! I wondered if Mama would save my spot in line. I counted them aloud. Seventy-five palm trees!

"I think we should claim a spot and never leave this place," I said.

Papa laughed. "Don't tempt me!" he answered with a chuckle. His eyes surveyed the thirsty throng of Israelites. "Look at them—total strangers visiting with one another. Children playing together like old friends. Peace reigns—at least for now."

The line moved slower than a slug. I licked my parched lips, but the wind dried them instantly.

A caravan must have visited this watering hole recently. I showed Saul a collection of deep round indentations—footprints left by camels. Saul made a game of stepping from camel print to camel print. "I'm a camel!" he sang.

At least a caravan knows exactly where it's headed and when it is due to arrive. Our days are beginning to blend into one big blur. I wish Moses would ask God for a shortcut.

After finally reaching the well and quenching our thirst, Papa and Ben filled deep containers with water. The water will last us for days if we're careful. I helped them haul it to a spot close to the clump of palms where Papa and Ben set up our tent. Mama didn't wait, though. She curled up on the edge of a grassy area. Our herds hungrily nibbled at anything green in sight.

Saul was not so content, though. He was holding his sides and groaning loud enough to wake the dead. "Didn't I caution you about gulping like a camel, Saul?" said Mama. She rubbed his bloated tummy and tried to talk him into lying down for a rest. He wouldn't hear of it.

I tried to distract Saul so he would stop whining. "Who wants to play a round of 'Guess What?'" Saul never tires of our special game.

"I do! I do!" he said, waving both arms.

I began: "I'm long and curvy, with two tiny eyes. Guess what I am?"

"Ben!" laughed Saul.

"No, goofy. It's a snake!" I pretended to be a reptile and chased him down.

Saul has matured in these early days of our journey—so much, in fact, I sometimes forget that he's still only five. The wilderness is not a playground. Snakes and creepy-crawly insects hide out, just waiting to pounce on passersby.

Saul has had to learn to stick close—something he never had to think much about back in Goshen. He doesn't get on my nerves as much anymore. I kind of feel sorry for him now.

Dear Friend,

NEWSFLASH! I got to bathe this evening. Well, not a real dip like we used to take in the Nile River, but it's as close to a real bath as I'll see out here. Grandmother guarded the tent opening so nobody would barge in, and I emerged so clean, my skin squeaked. "Who is this person?" she teased. "You smell so sweet!"

We took turns until everyone in our family had a chance to peel off layers of grime. Elim is proving to be a blessing in many ways.

Papa sat beneath a palm, waiting for his turn to wash. He and a group of friends are planning to meet under the tree again tomorrow. They're discussing our future, he says. What a difference for Papa, to be able to sit and freely discuss such things. The same strong hands that bear the scars of laboring for Pharaoh now express excitement for what lies ahead. It makes my heart glad.

Dear Friend,

This night is different from the other nights since our departure. The silence feels thick enough to slice. Everyone is sleeping soundly for once; everyone but me, that is.

It isn't worry that keeps me awake, but JOY. The night feels almost magical (although I dare not use that word with Grandmother around). It reminds me of another sleepless night back in Goshen. I remember unlatching the door and stepping outside for some fresh air. A full moon cast gleaming streaks of light, outlining the yellow blossoms on our acacia tree. It had seemed fitting to plant an acacia in Grandfather's memory. He had made many a gift from the hard wood of an acacia.

Tonight I think of Grandfather and his beloved blossoming spring trees, which don't grow here in the wilderness. If I squint my eyes just right, moonbeams shoot from the heavens and land in shimmering puddles at the foot of my sleeping mat.

Hot tears spill down my cheeks, running off my chin like a stream in search of the sea. Will the day come when I can think about Goshen without crying?

I must have dozed off. The cattle serenading our encampment woke me up. I stepped outside to investigate and saw why the livestock are so restless. Above the encampment the protective pillar of light dips and dances around the edges, its top licking

Bonnie Bruno

the sky like a hungry orange-yellow tongue. A cluster of palms forms a peaceful silhouette against the faded skyline.

The cool ground invites me to sift scratchy sand with my toes. I marvel at how the beautiful light touches everything in its path—tents, herds, and the refreshing springs of Elim. And I am amazed that the Creator of everything would make his presence known this way. I wonder, is this how Moses felt when he saw the burning bush?

Grumbles and Mumbles

Dear Friend,

I am harboring a secret—something too huge to put into words. I longed to climb a palm this morning and bellow to the crowd, "I met God last night!" Instead, I helped Mama by blowing red-hot cinders under our morning flatbread.

The pillar hung motionless today, like a tall cloudy statue, hemming us in. We move only when it moves. We camp wherever it stops. And we depend on it for direction until we reach Canaan—wherever that may be. Caanan. The name still sounds foreign to my Goshen-loving ears.

My head is like Mama's weaving loom—a mixture of questions noisily crisscrossing each other. The longer I wander this desert land, the less connected I feel to home. That makes me sad. It's becoming a double journey—a journey from and a journey to. And here in the land of in-between, I have no choice but to trust.

But before I share my experience, I want to be sure that I met God outside last night.

See how moody I can be? Why can't I be more like Tova? She

sets her mind on something and sticks to it. She doesn't waver. Some call that stubborn, but I call it determined.

And speaking of Tova, I wish she would set her mind on looking for me today.

Dear Friend,

Grandmother picked at her morning meal. Well, maybe "meal" is not the right word. We ate our bread and drank the small amount of milk our goats were able to supply. Some families don't have any milk at all, because the herds are not getting enough to eat. We are blessed today, but Papa predicts there may come a day when our faithful goats will no longer be able to produce.

I felt an arm around my shoulder, drawing me close. It was Mama. "How's my girl this morning?" she asked.

"Fine!" I had been waiting for the right moment to tell Mama about Tova, and this seemed as good a time as any. I took a deep breath. "Mama, Tova is acting strange. She's not herself at all." I explained how Tova seemed changed, distant. "She seemed almost embarrassed to be my friend."

Mama's expression turned thoughtful. "Well, sometimes people change, Sweetie," she said. "We've all been through a lot in a very short time. Maybe Tova needs some space to adjust. My guess is that before long you two will be chattering away like old times."

"But Mama, it's more than that," I insisted. "Something is terribly wrong, I just know it."

Mama cupped my chin and looked me straight in the eye. "Everything will be fine. Remember, you can't force friendship, Abigail."

I'm not trying to force our friendship; I just want it back to the way it was.

Dear Friend,

Ben's face has been pinched into a worried frown for days. It saddens me to see my carefree brother acting so gloomy.

"If I lose any more weight, my kneecaps are going to poke through the skin," he complained today. "I wake up hungry and go to bed hungry. How's a guy supposed to tend to the animals with so little to eat?"

Ben might as well have been talking to a stone wall. Grandmother was the only one who finally spoke up. "You call your mother's bread nothing? You're not the only one who's hungry, Ben."

Ben tried again. "Papa, what are we going to do if we don't find food soon? It's not like we can last forever out here!"

Papa's answer sent Ben stomping back to tend the herds. "Ben, if you can't say anything helpful, may God lock your jaws!"

End of conversation.

Dear Friend,

This lush green oasis grows on a person. I have been daydreaming of what it would be like to live here. I imagine neighborhoods cropping up all over Elim. Maybe I've soaked up too much sun or something.

I must not be the only one tired of life on the move, though. People are pleading with their elders to stay longer in Elim. The elders seem to be listening, too.

"What's the rush?" asked a nervous little man two tents over. "Surely another few days here in Elim is not going to disrupt our schedule."

His wife nodded in agreement. "Can't you see how weary we are? Our animals need a break. Our children need time to play and have fun. What does it matter if we reach Canaan a few days late?"

An elderly woman with long, wispy gray hair added her own thoughts. "We're not all young and energetic, you know. We can't go on day after day with so little food."

The elders of each tribe will be meeting soon with Moses, to present everyone's complaints to him. Moses, in turn, will cry out to God on our behalf.

Papa remains committed to focusing only on our blessings. He refuses to join the grumblers and mumblers. "Naysayers," he calls them.

"We're a pathetic band of complainers!" Papa scolded, loud enough for our neighbors to hear. "What have we become, fussy babies who need constant comforting?"

I was proud of Papa for speaking his mind today. Day in and day out, we have to put up with everyone's complaints. It gets tiring. And booooring, too.

Papa is right, Friend. It's easy to gripe about the weather or how far we have to walk. We complain about insects—and the hairy spider that invaded Papa's clothes pouch last night. We curse the darkness and then grumble when the tall pillar of light shines too brightly on our sleeping areas.

Lord, help me to look for ways to praise you. Give me a thankful heart.

Dear Friend,

Word traveled fast through the ranks. Families began packing their belongings and taking down their tents. It was time to say good-bye to Elim, our beautiful oasis. Like it or not, we were moving on. Anyone who decided otherwise would be left behind.

Papa heard rumors about certain families who want to turn back. "Such talk is pure nonsense!" he said. "Moses is trustworthy. He won't lead us astray. His instructions come straight from our God. Whoever turns back will not have the assurance of God's protection anymore. A dangerous journey awaits any who think they can make it back to Goshen on their own.

I hope Tova's family doesn't attempt such a trip.

Tova, my friend, where are you?

Papa and Ben slid the stretched animal hides off the tent frame. The hides stung my nose with their strong, musky odor. Our faithful ox waited as patiently as he waited other mornings. Who would have thought we could fit our most precious belongings into a few pouches? Mama's cooking pots, her loom, clothes, bedding, and a few mementos—all hung like prizes from the back of this four-legged servant. I scratched the scruff of his dusty neck. What would we do without you?

Mama hoisted the kneading bowl across my shoulders. "You're making us proud, Abigail," she said. "You're as much a servant as this beast—only a lot sweeter." She pecked my cheek to prove it.

We finished packing not a moment too soon—just as the pillar was easing forward. Farewell, Elim!

I feasted my eyes one last time on the soothing shade. Saul rolled one more time in the grass and jogged alongside us as we moved out. If I live to be one hundred and twenty, I doubt I'll ever find a place quite as welcoming as Elim.

Papa and Ben directed the herds with their staffs and prepared to follow. It was a comfort, knowing Papa was right behind us. A cloud before us, and a confident father behind us. Life on the open road could be worse, I suppose.

I grabbed Ben's hand and off we went. "Let the adventure begin," I said.

A woman nearby tossed me a dirty look. "*Hrrumph!* Some adventure!" She illustrated her protest by spitting on the ground.

Dear Friend,

I miss Elim already. Funny how easy it is to settle into a place. I won't go so far as to say it felt like home, but it sure was nice while it lasted. And green! I'd forgotten how gritty a pair of feet can get from shuffling along in the dirt.

The oasis was good for my body, but even better for my heart. I'll always remember how God touched me in that green oasis, out in the middle of nowhere.

Like Morning Dew

Dear Friend,

The Desert of Sinai stretches out before us. Lush, green Elim was a beauty to behold, but the wilderness presents a vast landscape of boring brown. The further we walked into it, the more my heart sank—and the more I thought about Moses. Upon his shoulders rests the job of leading thousands of men, women, and children to a land known only by God. Deep inside, is Moses afraid like the rest of us? Does his stomach flip whenever we round a bend and find the same nothingness waiting for us there? I wonder if he lies awake at night, wondering what he has gotten us into.

I hugged Grandmother today and felt something poke me. It was her ribs! She has been sharing her portion of bread with Mama, out of concern for the baby. I am going to keep an eye on Grandmother so she takes care of herself.

Mama has a round middle now. I patted her tenderly and made her promise to tell me when she feels the baby move.

"Relax," she said. "That won't happen for a while yet."

"Well, I hope she decides to kick for the first time when I'm nearby."

Mama grinned. She secretly wants another daughter, too. I can tell.

Dear Friend,

When I feel homesick for Goshen, I glance up at the cloud and feel comforted in ways I cannot even describe. By day, it's only a glance away. By night, it stands guard over our camp. And for night owls like me, it provides just the right amount of light for writing in a secret journal!

If I didn't have you, Friend, the words would build up inside me to the exploding point. If I ever find Tova again, I will talk her leg off. But for now, you are a wonderful keeper of my thoughts.

Dear Friend,

NEWSFLASH! Moses sent a message to the whole camp today. God has heard our complaints. He wants to remind us that he loves us and will provide everything we need.

Hurray! Maybe he'll lead us to an orchard filled with our favorite fruits and a garden overflowing with vegetables and grains and even flowers.

"Fat chance," said Ben.

Moses explained that God promises to bless us with bread every morning, enough for every single Israelite. That's a lot of bread!

And that's not all. Every evening, God is going to provide plenty of meat, too. In return, he expects us to stop complaining and murmuring. He wants us to give thanks when we receive it, and not wish for what we don't have.

Hmm-mm. That sounds simple enough.

Dear Friend,

NEWSFLASH! Our day ended on a bright note. God kept his word and provided meat this evening. That's right! A huge flock of quail circled overhead, flapping and carrying on as if they were sizing us up. They settled to the ground and lay there by the hundreds.

Ben thought it was hilarious. "Those quail have to be the dumbest birds on earth. They practically sailed into our cooking kettle."

Grandmother and I treated Mama to a night off. "Put your swollen feet up and relax, Susanna," said Grandmother. "Abigaily and I will take over the cooking tonight."

Dear Friend,

"Abigail! Pssst, Abigail! Get up!"

Ben's words cut through my sleep, jerking me into morning. How rude! Can't a person wake up on her own anymore?

"You've got to see this. Hurry!" insisted Ben.

My first glimpse of morning nearly sucked the breath out of me. The scorched brown wilderness of Sinai was dressed in gleaming white for as far as I could see. White splotches coated the ground like frost—just as God promised.

Ben jammed a piece of the white stuff into his mouth. "Taste it!" said Ben.

It tasted sweet as honey!

Father joined us outside to celebrate our discovery. "Susanna! Wake up!" yelled Papa. "We have bread from heaven, just as God promised!" he shouted.

Neighbors piled out of their tents, crying, "What is it? How'd it get here?"

Soon, a joyous chorus erupted, as their discovery sank in. "God has provided! God has provided! Sweet, sweet bread from heaven!" everyone sang. Nobody cared how they sounded; it was a melody of the heart—praise rising far above the desolate desert, to our Creator.

Papa hugged Mama. Mama hugged Ben and me. I hugged Saul. And Grandmother lifted her eyes toward heaven and cried happy tears.

"I knew God would provide!" she cried. "I knew it all along."

Moses called our people together as one, to give thanks for God's provision. Truly God is with us.

Dear Friend,

Uh-oh. There's trouble in the camp!

Moses is upset. He reminded our elders (who passed the message to everyone else) that we have not followed God's instructions for gathering manna (that's what we're calling the bread from heaven). "Each of you is to gather only what you need for your family," Moses reminded us. "Take about two quarts per person in your tent. Don't take any extra."

I'm glad I filled that other container with manna yesterday because today everyone is spying on each other. I've hidden the extra manna, and it'll last us a while yet. It's good for Mama to have plenty to eat. After all, she is eating for two now, right? Surely God understands, doesn't he?

Certain people (like the man with the nine children) ignore the rule because they're just plain greedy. I saw him stuff manna in three different containers this morning—even after hearing God's warning.

Moses calls such sneakiness a sign of distrust. People who break the rules are not trusting God to provide our daily manna, he says. From now on, God wants us to leave any extra manna on the ground—or share it with others who were not able to gather enough for themselves. If everyone sticks to the rules, there will be plenty of manna for us all.

Like Morning Dew

Dear Friend,

This morning I opened the other container of manna with plans to surprise Mama with an extra portion at breakfast. A horrible shock awaited me: Filthy maggots wriggled in and out of the manna like guests at a feast. I gagged and wretched and took off running to the edge of the nearest gully. There I dumped the manna—container and all—into a deep abyss. I hurried back to camp, hoping that nobody saw me. That's what I get for disobeying God. He promised to provide our daily bread, and what did I do? I tried to outsmart him. How dumb is that?

But I wasn't the only dumb one. A revolting stench drifted across our encampment like a giant finger, drawing attention to the families who broke the manna-gathering rule. Imagine waking up and planning a big breakfast, only to discover wriggly maggots nibbling away at your manna supply.

That's what happened this morning to the man with the nine kids. He is embarrassed and enraged. I can only imagine what his tent smells like! Everyone who disobeyed and greedily gathered more than their fair share will have to face the consequences. I feel sorry for his children, who will go hungry today.

Grandmother hates cheating. "Next time he'll not try to bend God's law," she says sternly.

I didn't tell her about my little lesson.

Dear Friend,

What day could be more perfect than today? After filling our bellies with manna, neighbors chatted with neighbors and total strangers struck up conversations.

Ben and I searched for small pieces of wood—anything to set aside for our next campfire. Without a fire, we couldn't cook, and

Mama has big plans for tonight, she says. Papa loaned me an empty pouch, which I slung over my shoulder.

We filled our pouch with twigs and were turning to go when a couple of kids leapt out from behind a bramble bush. "Abigail!" I heard someone call. "Abby!"

Tova!

First manna—and now this? The moment was too much to contain. I burst into tears.

Tova hugged me long and hard. "I've missed you so much, Abby. Where are you camped, anyway?"

I pointed over to Mama, who was busy packing for another day on the move. "Come on," I said, grabbing Tova's hand. "Mama would love to see you."

"I can't right now, Abigail. I have to take this home first."

Home. It sounded strange to hear that word again. The wilderness hardly feels like home, but I suppose that is what it has become. Tova held a container of manna. "I found extra out there in the clearing," she said. "Mama needs more nourishment if she's going to get well. Come home with me, Abigail—please? It'll take only a minute."

"Okay," I agreed. "It'll be fun to surprise your mother after all this time."

Tova's camp was not far from mine. "Mother, we have a surprise visitor. Look who's here."

Tova spoke softly to the thin, pale woman huddled over the remains of a campfire.

Mother? But how could it be? This was not the woman I remembered. She stared at me through distant, hollow eyes. Sharp cheekbones pressed against pale, nearly transparent skin.

"Abigail, dear," she said, reaching for my hand. "How nice to see you." Her icy touch drove chills up my arm. How could anyone feel that cold on such a sunny morning? I couldn't take my eyes off her, but I didn't have the heart to ask questions, either.

Tova unwrapped the container of manna. "Here, Mother. I found more. You can nibble on it all day if you'd like. There'll be plenty more where that came from tomorrow."

I convinced Tova to stop by my camp when she was done with her chores. I'm waiting for her now.

Dear Friend,

Tova came, but it wasn't as happy a time as I thought it would be. It started off that way but changed quickly.

"Well, well, well! Look who's here!" cried Mama. She kissed and hugged Tova like a long-lost daughter.

"We thought you'd taken a wrong turn somewhere out there," joked Papa.

My parents had watched Tova grow up. She was like one of their own. It felt like a family reunion.

"And how's your mother? Father? And little David—he must be half grown by now."

Tova's gaze fell to the ground. "He ... uh ... David died three days before we left Goshen."

My world stood still. I heard myself gasp. "Tova—NO!"

"Poor boy coughed for days. It finally sucked the last breath right out of him," she said, her voice breaking.

"I am so sorry, so very sorry," said Mama, gathering Tova into a warm embrace. "I wish we'd known sooner. I so wish we had known."

"And your parents—how are they faring? What can we do to help?"

"Sad," said Tova. "They're both sad and homesick. Very, very homesick."

Why, God? Why didn't you make David well? Why does this family have to suffer so?

When Tova left, Mama said, "Please give your family my love. And tell them our hearts are broken at this tragic news."

I walked her to the edge of the clearing. "Turn and wave as soon as you get back to camp," I said.

I thought of the days when we would wave to each other from the clearing between our houses back in Goshen.

Heal their broken hearts, I prayed. And I wept.

Dear Friend,

It has taken days for me to write again. My head has been reeling from the awful news Tova shared with me. Now I understand her absence. I understand everything—and I hurt for her.

I am getting anxious to reach the so-called Promised Land. I am eager to call someplace home again. I imagine living in a place close to Tova's house. Now that I have found my best friend, I do not intend to lose her again!

Dear Friend,

We were on the march again today. I walked alongside Mama, Grandmother, and Saul for much of the day today—a determined foursome. All the while, thoughts of Tova's loss kept crowding for a front-row seat in my head. I held Saul's hand like I never wanted to let it go.

How can God give so freely, yet take so suddenly? Are any of us safe from sorrow?

Moses knows every twist and turn through the wilderness. Hopefully he knows a short route to Canaan, too. So far, we keep following the same brown path to nowhere.

At one point, a group of roving shepherds paused to watch us pass. I wonder what they thought of our colorful parade.

If Only

Dear Friend,

We fried strips of tender quail and patted the last of our manna supply into little cakes. Grandmother heated our trusty baking stone over the fire, and then spread the cakes on top to bake.

"Mannacakes," I said, rolling the word off my tongue. "Yum! We've invented a new treat, Grandmother."

I counted the little round cakes—twenty-two in all. "We have more than enough food for the six of us. Could I invite Tova to dinner?"

"It's fine with me," said Grandmother. "In fact, let's invite her whole family. We haven't shared a meal with guests since our last night in Goshen. It'll do us all good."

Papa agreed. "Ben, why don't you go with Abigail. It's close to dark, and I don't want your sister wandering around by herself."

Late-afternoon shadows crisscrossed our path in an eerie display. "Tova is camped somewhere up here," I said, pointing straight ahead.

A smoky haze drifted over the massive encampment. "Yum!

Smell that?" asked Ben. "It smells like everyone's using the same recipe tonight."

"Hmm-mm, let me guess," I joked back. "Could it be quail?"

When we reached Tova's camp, she and her father were trying to coax a stubborn little fire along. They were more than happy to desert their duties and join us for dinner. I sensed a hesitation in her mother's voice, though. "We'd love if you'd come, too," I said, kneeling by where she sat. "Mama is so looking forward to visiting with you—like old times."

"Please, Mother?" begged Tova. "It won't be any fun if you stay behind."

When Tova and her parents reached our camp Saul bellowed, "Where's David? I want to teach him how to play a new game!"

I could have wrung his neck, but it wasn't his fault. He doesn't understand that his little friend won't be coming back. Tova's mother dabbed at her eyes while Mama tried to console her. We ate in awkward silence, interrupted only by an occasional discussion between Papa and Tova's father—cattle and goat talk, mostly. Grandmother filled the silence by offering to refill everyone's plates.

It was not a fun evening.

After dinner, Tova's mother sat across from Mama in a private area where they could talk. Mama hates anyone to suffer alone. Tova and I played a game of tag with Saul—his favorite pastime.

Thankfully, he didn't ask about David again.

After darkness closed in, Saul headed for the campfire, where Ben, Papa, and Tova's father sat around talking about their high hopes for life in the Promised Land.

I was glad to have time alone with Tova—finally. We avoided the topic of her brother. When she's ready, I figure she'll talk about it. Instead, I asked about Nan.

"Hey, where's what's-her-name—the girl you were with the day you ran off?"

Tova's face reddened. "Oh, she found a friend her own age. Nan's younger than us, you know."

"I know," I said. "And bossier, too."

I didn't want the evening to end. We still had so much catching up to do. "Next time you can come to my house," Tova said when we parted.

"House?" I teased. "It looks more like a tent to me."

"You know what I mean," said Tova. It was beautiful to see my friend smile after all she had been through.

"Wave to me when you reach your camp, and I'll wave back," I reminded her.

Dear Friend,

If only Tova's brother had not gotten sick. He and Saul could have run around making noise and getting into mischief, as always. If only we had not left Goshen, Tova and I would be leaning against the old oak, swapping secrets instead of calling this desolate wilderness home.

If only Grandfather were still here, I'd have someone to talk to, who could figure out my confusion.

I don't understand why some people grow wrinkled and gray-haired, but others leave this world almost as soon as they arrive. And how is it that I have two healthy brothers, but Tova's David was taken from her so soon?

If only … If only … That question wears me out. For tonight, at least, I will trust that God has a reason for everything. Otherwise, why would I be writing in my secret journal from this breezy tent in the middle of who-knows-where?

Dear Friend,

We have a neighbor who complains about God's choice of meat. He runs his mouth from dawn to dusk.

"So, every single evening, we're going to feast on quail, quail, quail?" he said, rolling his eyes. "Why can't God send some wild turkeys or chickens once in a while? Is that too much to ask?"

"Life is filled with rule-benders and complainers," said Grandmother, wagging her finger. "His children are going to grow up as infidels!"

To chase away boredom, we've thought of clever ways to prepare our bread from heaven. This morning, for example, I helped Mama grind a bowlful of manna then mold it into soft dumplings. We boiled the clumps gently for a few minutes and—ta-da!— "Papa's Porridge" was born.

Papa thought the porridge tasted nutty. He's easy to please and said he didn't even notice the lumps.

If only we had some onions or carrots to add to the manna, what a delicious dish we could make for dinner.

I like coming up with names for each manna meal. So far we've served "Susanna's Surprise" and "Abigail's Amazing Manna-cakes." By the time we reach Canaan, we'll have enough manna recipes for a family collection.

Time for a poetry break!

Manna Madness

Manna, manna every morning—
Lord, it's getting awfully boring!
Manna pudding, manna gruel …
Life with manna sure is cruel!

Evening quail and mannawiches
(Papa calls them "heaven's riches");
Manna fried and manna steamed
How I crave a bowl of beans!

Dear Friend,

We are moving deeper into the wilderness of Sinai. The terrain looks different from the wilderness of Shur. A ridge of mountains lies on one side, and deep gullies throughout. It's especially hard on Papa and Ben, as they try to keep our animals from running astray or falling into the crevices.

It's almost as hard for those of us back at the encampment who are surrounded by grumbling neighbors.

"If God can create a mountain range, why can't he create a new flavor of manna?"

"If I see another quail, I'm going to scream!"

"I'd rather be back in Egypt! At least we had fresh fruits and vegetables once in a while."

Gripe, gripe, gripe. I am so sick of hearing it! Do people think their nonstop complaints are going to change our menu?

Who wouldn't love a bowl of fresh steamed vegetables? I'd even trade a whole day's worth of manna for a nice juicy melon!

But here's what I have to look forward to this week:

Sunday: Manna & Quail
Monday: Manna & Quail
Tuesday: Manna & Quail
Wednesday: Manna & Quail
Thursday: Manna & Quail
Friday: Manna & Quail
Saturday: Manna & Quail

Father calls our people fickle. He says, "How easy it is to forget how far God has brought us—how he protected us from plagues, parted the great sea, and provided food and water all along. How dare we complain!"

Dear Friend,

The sky is purple-black tonight and filled with twinkly jewels. I've not seen a starry night like this in ages. Between starlight and the glow from God's pillar of fire, our tent is bathed in the Lord's presence tonight.

Papa's no-murmuring rule prevents me from speaking my mind in the daytime. He is fed up with grumblers. So I store my complaints inside my head, where nobody else can hear them.

Well, nobody except God and you, Friend.

Soon I will be thirteen, and I don't want to sound like a spoiled child. How does someone like me learn to let go and trust God for what I cannot see? Is it possible to focus on the Promised Land instead of today's problems?

Consider the Stars

Dear Friend,

I awoke to a howling sound this morning—a commotion coming from two tents away. Papa ran to see what was wrong. A deadly scorpion had bitten a two-year-old girl!

Oh, no! The wilderness harbors scorpions, too?

I glanced over at Saul, who slept straight through the ruckus. He looked sweet and innocent, lying there with hair spilling across his face. I want to protect him from anything that would harm him. I will watch him more closely from now on.

Papa says we can't afford to let our guard down. The wilderness is full of creatures that aren't used to sharing their home with humans. Snakes, spiders, fleas, and now scorpions. And those are just one fraction of the list.

Dear Friend,

A dry southern khamsin blew in about mid-morning. It raged with such force, many of our neighbors watched in horror as tents ripped loose from their moorings and flew halfway across the camp. We raced for a gully and laid low until the sandstorm passed. Saul clung to me like a second skin, burying his face against my back.

My face stings from the force of flying sand, but I'm more fortunate than the animals. Dozens of our goats and sheep ran off in a wild-eyed frenzy! Papa says he doubts whether we'll be able to find them. Thank goodness our Sassy is a homebody. She didn't budge an inch. Papa found her moo-ing at the base of a hill where she had gotten herself tangled in a row of sticker bushes.

Now it's raining—not a gentle spring rain, but a torrential downpour. Nomads who brave this harsh weather and terrain tell us that spring rains often last for days! It runs off the land into parched, cracked *wadis*—gullies that fill to the top with rainwater. Sometimes the water overflows and floods the land.

Dear Friend,

Will this rain never stop? We're surrounded by a soggy, slippery, muddy mess. Even though it's dry (and kind of cozy) inside our tent, a dampness hangs in the air. These animal hides are starting to stink!

The worst part, though, is that our fire went out. This is the first night we weren't able to roast quail. My stomach is rumbling a steady reminder that I haven't eaten since this morning.

I'm keeping one eye on the pillar of cloud. So far it has not budged. Surely God won't make us stay here in a flooded wilderness, will he? Would he bring us all this way to watch us drown?

Dear Friend,

NEWSFLASH! The rains have stopped.

NEWSFLASH! My heart aches for the family two tents over. Their little girl has died from the scorpion's sting. Her mourning relatives fill the air with wails. It is a cry heard much too often in this desolate place. Many will die before our journey is over. Please, God, not my family!

Today is the sixth day of the week. When we gathered our bread from heaven today, we gathered twice as much as normal. But don't worry. These are Moses' instructions. God will keep the extra portion fresh so we won't have to gather food tomorrow, on the Sabbath. God wants us to complete our baking today, too, so we won't have to work on his holy day.

Dear Friend,

We rested today—and what a welcome rest it was. I'm glad that we must honor the Sabbath day to keep it holy.

The ground is damp from the downpour. I wanted to bathe, but the closest wadi is so full of swift-flowing water, it would have been too risky to venture in. So, I will try to ignore the fact that I am beginning to smell more like a goat than a girl. Mama didn't seem to care about my odor. She sneaked up behind me today and grabbed me in a gigantic hug.

Dear Friend,

I have lost track of time here in the great wilderness, and Mama had to remind me of something special: Tomorrow is my birthday!

We usually don't celebrate birthdays, but it is my thirteenth birthday, and Papa wants to bless me. I feel cherished.

I am looking forward to flaunting my age in front of Ben, too. Beginning tomorrow, he will no longer be the only teenager in our family.

"I guess that means you won't get away with acting childish anymore," he teased.

"No, it means that you won't get away with acting like you know everything," I corrected him.

I hope Ben and I will always be close. He keeps me laughing.

Dear Friend,

Mama tossed a handful of chopped dates into our manna mixture this morning. She had been saving them for my special day. She asked me to close my eyes and surprised me with a heart-shaped manna cake she designed herself. The moment was so sweet, I felt like I might cry.

Papa directed me to a place of honor next to him. After we ate, he talked about the day I was born. "You came squalling into the world and captured our hearts," he said. "That is why we named you Abigail, which means 'gives joy.'"

Everyone took turns naming one thing they appreciate about me. Ben laughed. "You have so many wonderful qualities, dear sister," he said sarcastically, "it's hard to narrow them down to just one." Papa didn't let him off so easily, and finally Ben said, "You're honest. If I ask you for an opinion, you don't just tell me what I want to hear. You tell me what you really think." He glanced away, and I think I saw him blush. "If you weren't my sister, I'd choose you for a friend, Abigail."

Saul said he likes the stories I tell him.

Mama likes my heart. She called it "soft and caring."

And Papa—well, Papa thinks I am turning into a good cook. (Ha! He wasn't around the day I forgot to pluck the quail's feathers before roasting it.)

I think I could sleep for a week if I set my mind to it. It is the end of a perfect day—the Sabbath and my birthday. Today I feel at home, even here in the wilderness of Sinai.

Dear Friend,

We've pitched our tent in Rephidim. The long trip is catching up with us, and many of us are weak-kneed and dizzy. Our animals will die soon if we can't find fresh water.

People are growing more impatient every day. This is not the journey they expected when they fled Egypt! A group of men huddled in a semicircle, exchanging heated remarks about Moses. (My old eavesdropping habit came in handy.)

"He isn't taking charge," barked a man in his early twenties. "We're a nation without a real leader."

"He's slow with words, not a good spokesman at all," agreed his friend. "That's why his brother Aaron has to deliver half his messages!"

"Well, Moses had better watch his step, or he's going to find himself dodging stones!" declared another.

The discussion continued well into the night. By morning, it had spread to other circles of debaters, who decided to approach Moses with their complaints.

Dear Friend,

I've got to quit biting my nails! It's a nervous habit and not at all ladylike, says Grandmother. It's also a sign of worry, which I promised I wasn't going to do anymore.

Papa is concerned about the uproar around here. He says that Moses doesn't deserve this kind of treatment. I'm worried that someone will try to overpower him or organize others to disobey his leadership. Worse yet—I'm afraid that an angry mob may try to kill him.

I hope you're paying attention, Lord.

Dear Friend,

Parents are yelling at their restless children. Neighbors are picking fights with each other and swearing to get even. It's as if we've all gone crazy! Papa says we can't continue much longer without water.

"Life will only get harder until we learn to listen and obey— really obey," says Papa.

But how can anyone listen when they feel such thirst? And why would God stop his tall pillar of light at a place like Rephidim where there isn't any water?

The loud-mouthed man camped next to us bellowed to a neighbor across the way, "Moses is an imposter! We've all been duped. How could we have been so stupid, following him to this godforsaken place?"

Dear Friend,

Night has fallen, but the camp is far from quiet. Three times now, I've heard the sound of people running back and forth in a frustrated quest to gather news. I also overheard voices near the edge of the pasture, making plans to overthrow Moses! Something big is going to happen. I can feel it in my bones.

I am learning that God's ways are not our ways.

Instead of wiping out the evil ones, God had a better plan. He instructed Moses to take a few elders with him as witnesses. They went ahead of our congregation where God led them to a rock. He told Moses to strike it with his staff.

Are you ready for this? Water gushed from that rock with such force, it ran in streams across the land!

The same crowd who wanted to hurt Moses a few hours ago now cheered. Water in the desert—who would have thought such a thing possible?

My dear old grandmother was not one bit surprised, though. "God is willing and able. He never changes. All he asks for is our obedience and trust."

Dear Friend,

Sleep is nowhere to be found tonight. I slipped over to the entrance of our tent and crouched there in the dark. The sky was purple-black, filled with stars too numerous to count.

My thoughts turned to another night long ago, when Grandfather and I laid on our backs under a twinkling purple-black sky. "Consider the stars," he said, stretching his arms toward the heavens. "God numbers each star and sees every one that falls. Nothing escapes his notice, Abigail. Nothing!"

My mind could not wrap itself around such a thought. "But what if God blinks?" I wondered.

Grandfather laughed the way only he could laugh—from the belly up. "I'm sure he doesn't miss a thing, even if he blinks," he laughed. "And if God notices the course of every single star, you can be sure that he sees each step you and I take, too."

The pillar of light flickered, pulling me back to this sleepless night in Rephidim. Its flame sent a warm, golden glow across our encampment.

God is awake. I feel it in my bones. He provided all that we needed today.

And if Grandfather was right, God already knows what tomorrow will bring.

Thunderclaps and a Trumpet Call

Dear Friend,

We have pitched our tents at the base of Mount Sinai. The peak looms tall and proud, higher than any of the other mountains in the wilderness. Moses announced that we will be staying here until further notice. Hurray! It'll be a treat to wake up in the same camp for awhile.

Thorny bushes stretch across the valley like wild bouquets. It was a challenge to find an empty spot big enough for our tent.

Mama and Grandmother have been chattering nonstop since we arrived. They welcome the opportunity to rest here in the shadow of the mountain. Mother set up her beloved loom and has unpacked colorful thread she brought all the way from Goshen. She has been promising to make me a new robe. Grandmother says if I behave myself (wink!), she might even embroider flowers around the edges of the sleeves.

Dear Friend,

I'm grateful for a chance to feel rooted for awhile. It's not that I mind the journey so much anymore; I just love the parts when we get to stop and take a deep breath.

The mountain looks awesome at night, majestic. The bulrushes give off a strong odor I've never smelled before. They look like an ideal place for a snake to seek shelter. And speaking of snakes, I hope we don't find any surprises in the kneading bowl tomorrow morning.

This morning I slipped out of bed to collect our day's supply of manna. I wanted to surprise Mama, who has been sleeping fitfully lately. That silly baby keeps somersaulting when she should be slumbering!

I was surprised to discover other early risers already returning with their day's ration of manna. As I stooped to gather handfuls of the sweet, white stuff, something caught my eye: a herd of gazelles grazing nearby. I have never seen such beautiful animals. Golden and sleek, they tipped their horned heads down to nibble hungrily on the bulrushes.

Several of the gazelles sensed my presence and froze in place. They gazed through gentle eyes ringed with patches of fluffy white fur. I can't wait to describe the scene to Ben. He and Caleb have been exploring the area around our encampment, and spotted a fox last night. Ben thinks the fox is hunting for rats. That's one piece of information I would rather forget. Rats—in our camp? Yeccch!

Dear Friend,

I have been so excited, I can hardly sit still. All day I have been anticipating this time when I could curl up on my bed and write the latest baby news. Mama says the baby is kicking more each day. She even laid my hand against her tummy and (are you ready for this?) I felt a strong THUMP! Then another. And another!

"Only a baby girl could be that restless," said Grandmother.

Oh, how I hope she's right!

Tova showed up in the middle of our exciting moment. I feel almost guilty being this happy. Tova lost a sibling, but in a few months I will be gaining one. God subtracts from one family and adds to another, yet loves each of us the same. It is one of life's mysteries.

Mama longs for this child to be born in Canaan. She thinks a sister or brother would be a perfect Welcome Home present to the whole family.

Tova and I scrambled through the maze of thorn bushes to gather pieces of starter wood for our campfires today. It gave us a chance to talk.

I am so disappointed, I don't know where to begin. I feel sad for Tova. She is like a worrisome old woman. The friend who used to cheer me has all but given up on ever reaching the Promised Land.

"Think about it, Abigail," she said. "If Moses was really God's appointed leader, wouldn't he have led us on a smarter route out of Egypt? If he had taken us by way of the coast, we would have arrived in Canaan in five or six days. We'd be tending our new gardens by now instead of camped in this scorched wasteland."

How quickly Tova forgets that a shortcut might have ended in tragedy. If Moses had ignored God's instructions, Pharaoh's army might have dragged us back to Egypt, or worse—slaughtered us on the spot. I reminded her of how hard our fathers slaved in Egypt, but she seems to have forgotten their struggles.

"My father says it wasn't so bad. Not compared to this, at least," she said, pointing to our dreary surroundings. Just a few months ago, I'd never have expected to hear such talk from my best friend.

One thing I've learned out here in the wilderness: I can't force anyone to believe the way I do—not even a close friend. When I tried to remind her about the pillar of cloud and fire, she only shrugged.

"You have a big imagination, Abigail. It looks like a plain ol' cloud to me."

Tova has an answer for every topic, from manna and quail to the rock that gushed water. She exhausts me.

We parted with a hug, but my heart feels heavier than ever for her. We are growing apart, and I don't know how to fix it.

Dear Friend,

Life has fallen into a routine. It feels good to sink shallow roots for a change. We're keeping busy; no idle hands here! Mama gave me a tiny linen baby garment, and Grandmother is teaching me how to embroider tiny pastel flowers around the neckline and hem. It's fun to sit in a circle—three generations of us—and make baby clothes together. My stitches are not as fine as Grandmother's, but I am learning.

"My baby sister won't mind," I said with a wink.

"It's best to keep an open mind, Abigail," said Grandmother. "As much as you'd like a sister, God might bless you with a precious baby brother instead."

I'd better not describe what I'd think of a "blessing" like that. Two brothers are quite enough, thank you very much.

Mama discovered nibble-marks on the lid of our manna-gathering container! Rats! Fortunately, those rascal rodents weren't able to chew their way inside. Papa says God prevented them from reaching our precious manna.

God has promised to keep on supplying "bread from heaven." Even the most persistent rat cannot thwart God's plan for his people.

Thunderclaps and a Trumpet Call

Dear Friend,

Moses left today to meet God on the mountain. Sinai is a rugged climb, even for a young man like Ben, but Moses is far from young. What if he falls and injures himself? I shudder at the thought of journeying the rest of the way to Canaan without our faithful leader. Papa assured me that God will strengthen Moses and enable him to endure the climb.

Down here in the valley, I keep hoping we'll discover wild vegetables, but so far, we're doomed to eat the same foods day in and day out. My taste buds yearn for a warm slice of Grandmother's famous caraway bread and a steaming bowl of lamb-vegetable stew—Mama's specialty.

Sometimes I gag at the thought of eating another bite of manna and quail, but without God's provision, I know that we would have perished long ago. So yes, I am grateful.

Dear Friend,

NEWSFLASH! Moses has returned from his mountaintop meeting. God gave him a message so life-changing, we must first wash our clothes and cleanse our hearts before we can receive it. Everyone has two days to prepare. We must set aside all work and spend our time praying and thinking of God's goodness to us.

And that's not all. Any person or animal that ventures near the mountain, or even touches a rock near its base, will be struck dead. (I told Mama we had better tie Saul to a bush!)

Dear Friend,

I barely slept a wink last night. It is almost dawn on the third day—the day God plans to meet with us. A thick cloud covers Mount Sinai. Our sheep are bleating nervously, as if they sense a storm approaching. I have no idea what to expect. My stomach is churning as I strain to see the top of the great mountain through the doorway of our tent. I wish Papa and Mama would wake Grandmother and the others. How can they sleep with such an important event looming?

Dear Friend,

I will remember the day of the Lord's appearing for as long as I live. Fire spewed from the mountain like a crimson torch as God's presence descended into our midst. Flashes of lightning zigzagged across daybreak! Thunderclaps rumbled and roared through the valley! The whole mountain quaked, followed by a trumpet blast so loud, our entire congregation trembled. Saul covered his ears and buried his face against Papa's leg.

Moses called us to join him at the base of the mountain. There we waited in spotless clothes, our hearts prepared for that sacred moment.

God spoke in a booming voice, while thunder continued to roll across the plains. He declared that he alone is our one true God—the faithful one who has delivered us from the hands of the Egyptians

People turned their backs to the mountain, suddenly aware of their sins. Standing in God's presence, we recalled all the ways we had wronged each other. We remembered our grumbling and mumbling and times of disobedience.

Moses understood our feelings and calmed the crowd. Then he disappeared into a thick, dark cloud to meet privately with God.

Now a hush hangs over our camp. It is a stillness I've not heard since the early days of this journey. Even the animals seem more at rest tonight.

Today at the base of the mountain, I felt God's presence. I know I didn't imagine it, Friend. He was there! So holy was that moment, I had to turn away. It gives me chills to think about it.

How Much Farther

Dear Friend,

We waited for Moses to emerge from the clouds, but soon everyone gave up and returned to their tents.

Papa tried to assure us that everything would be alright. "Moses will return when God is finished speaking to him and not a minute before."

I begged Papa to intervene. "How can we just sit here and do nothing? Moses could have fallen into a rocky crevice and be bleeding, Papa! Or, maybe he was overcome by smoke on the mountaintop."

"Abigail, don't you ever listen?" scoffed Ben. "Moses said that if we so much as touch a stone at the base of the mountain, we will die. Nobody can rescue him. We don't dare go near the mountain."

I tried to stay busy with everyday chores today. This morning Saul tagged along to gather our supply of manna. He thought it was a game and helped me fill the container in record time.

My steps felt lighter this morning, my heart hopeful. I have witnessed bitter water cleansed. I have seen God provide manna every morning and fowl every evening, just as he promised he would. Every dawn, I see his presence strong and true, as the pillar of cloud welcomes a new day. And every night, God's pillar flickers its protective flame over our encampment.

I am sure Moses is safe.

Grandfather was right; God watches over our comings and our goings and everything in between. He supplies relief when we need it—even when we do not deserve it.

I don't pretend to understand it. I just believe it.

Dear Friend,

Tova is in one of her moods again, worried that we may end up stuck in this thorn-covered valley forever.

"I thought Canaan was supposed to be a land flowing with milk and honey. Do you see anything except thistles, Abigail? How much longer will we have to sleep in these stinking tents?"

Tova does have a point. It has been three months since we said goodbye to Goshen. Three whole months! It seems only fitting that a Promised Land would boast shade trees, wildflowers, and cool, bubbling streams—wouldn't it? Would God take this long to deliver a promise?

Dear Friend,

I'm sleepy, but I have something important to say. Call it a confession if you like. Not so long ago, a yearning for Goshen hung around my heart like a heavy stone. I doubted whether Moses had really heard from God. I thought for sure he was leading us astray, like stupid sheep.

Every now and then, a part of me aches for the familiar—the smell of the Nile River on a warm afternoon, the sound of golden orioles exchanging morning greetings, and the glow of a golden sunset bathing the west wall of our house. Goshen will forever capture a special corner of my heart. It's a big part of who I am.

But it's just as important to go on. We've come too far to stray off course.

Lord, thank you for leading us by day and refreshing us by night. And please watch over Moses.

Dear Friend,

Two weeks have passed since Moses disappeared into the cloud on Mount Sinai. Papa reminds us that Moses will return only when the time is right.

Some people aren't as patient as Papa, though. Something strange is happening while our leader is away. Papa says that our people are slipping into idolatry—worshiping a false God. Moses' own brother, Aaron, issued a call for people to turn in their gold earrings. The earrings will be melted and used to create a graven image—a golden calf.

"Heathens!" hissed Grandmother. "Can they not wait a single hour for God to complete his work?"

Troublemakers are running about, stirring up doubt. "Moses should have returned long before now," they say.

"Some leader, huh? Maybe he ran off and left us to die out here."

Others are calling for a new leader who will help us complete the march to Canaan. "We can't camp in this godforsaken wilderness forever," they remind everyone.

Mama is growing more uncomfortable with each passing week. It won't be long before my baby sister will be wearing the beautiful gown I embroidered for her.

Dear Friend,

Tova and her mother stopped by today for a visit and admired our baby clothes.

Tova is not in favor of waiting for Moses' return. In fact, she doesn't think there is anything wrong with the people who are stirring up rebellion.

"I'm sick and tired of dealing with these thorn bushes and fleas. We've been camped out here for weeks, Abigail, and for what? Nobody seems to know. I say we need to keep moving, or we'll never reach the Promised Land."

As we parted, I couldn't help but notice that Tova was not wearing her usual small gold ear hoops. Neither was her mother wearing any jewelry. My heart sank. Tova has given up on Moses, but I wonder, has she also deserted God? Has she turned her gold earrings over to Aaron?

Dear Friend,

A golden calf stands high above an altar, glistening in the sunlight. People claim that the graven image really represents God and that it helps them to worship something they can see. Papa says they're making excuses to feast and party while Moses is away. They're even sacrificing to the golden calf, the way Egyptians have done since ancient times.

In my heart, I know this should not be happening. God is God—he doesn't live in man-made images. We can't capture him by melting gold earrings and molding a golden calf. What an insult to our Creator!

Didn't they learn anything when God came down the mountain to meet with us? Have they forgotten how the earth quaked and the thunder rolled?

Dear Friend,

I discovered a fellow sojourner this morning, a fuzzy caterpillar wriggling across the spiky branch of an acacia tree. Every so often, it would pause to rest. I thought of the light surrounding God's appearance on Mount Sinai, and how we marveled at that amazing event.

Someday I will not be a traveler anymore. But for now, I must make the best of it, like this lone caterpillar inching up the tree.

My little brother has made an announcement. "I'm going home!" he said.

He says he's tired of playing tag among the thistles. He's scared to death of rats. He wants to haul his little collection of toys back to the field behind our home in Goshen and plans to dip his toes in the stream again. And he wants Mama to go with him so she can make a big pot of lamb curry on her stove out in the courtyard.

I talked Saul into going on a walk with me. We searched for the caterpillar. It was nowhere to be found. Gone. I was ready to give up when Saul let out a whoop. "There he is! Right there, chewing on a leaf."

Every traveler needs a break—even this fuzzy creature. I wonder if he traveled a long distance to nibble on the leaf today?

Dear Friend,

NEWSFLASH! Moses returned from the mountain, lugging two tablets of stone. Written on each stone are the ten laws God gave to our people. The writing came from God's own hand, permanently carved into the heavy tablets.

Our camp changed during the forty days and nights while Moses was away. Continuous singing and dancing now surrounds the golden calf. It is a never-ending party as some of our people lift praise to this false god.

When Moses saw what the people were doing, he flew into a rage and tossed the stone tablets to the ground.

I ran for the safety of our tent. Papa and Ben watched from a distance as Moses knocked the golden calf over and rolled it into a red-hot fire.

"Did the golden calf rise up to save you?" roared Moses. "Can you not wait a single hour on our God?"

Dear Friend,

The golden calf burnt into a fine powder. Moses dumped the remains in the water. Then he challenged everyone to make a choice. In a booming voice, he told us that we are either for God or against him. There is no in-between! My knees shook, and I could feel my heart beating so hard, I thought everyone must surely hear it.

Papa whispered, "It's decision time," and in one swift motion, my entire family stepped forward, along with thousands of other cheering Israelites, to publicly declare our love for our God. Everyone else—those who refused to repent of their sin of idolatry—were slain—around three thousand in all.

Imagine that, three thousand people! Parents and children, with hopes and dreams just like me! Three thousand people who somehow lost their way in the wilderness and turned their backs on God.

Why wouldn't they listen? Why were parents willing to give up everything, including their hope of reaching God's Promised Land, to worship a dumb golden idol that couldn't speak or forgive or love them back? Why, Lord? Why?

I pointed to the pillar of cloud, which still hovered in the same place as always, right over our camp. "Look!" I cried out. "Some of our people turned away, but God is still here with us! He is as faithful as ever."

In my heart, I know that's true, but how will I ever erase the terrible sights and sounds of this day? If only I had the power to turn back the time! I wonder how many of those slain today would make a different choice if they had another chance.

Will tomorrow bring an uprising or will our nation prove itself worthy of God's blessing? How much farther must we wander before we reach our Promised Land?

Hope!

Dear Friend,

Hundreds of camps stand silent and deserted, their tents and cooking utensils untouched since that fateful morning of judgment. Carved wooden animals await the return of children. Kneading bowls lie empty near cold fire pits, still wrapped in their protective cloths. Every person who worshiped the golden calf is now gone—forever!

How can people trust God so easily one day, yet turn their backs on him the next? Why would anyone choose to worship a statue made of simple earthly material? The golden calf couldn't guide us safely through this wilderness. It couldn't hear and answer our prayers.

Dear Friend,

A spine-chilling thought haunts me. It is too terrible to say aloud, but too serious to ignore. I haven't seen Tova in over a week. I'm afraid she and her parents might have been among the group who danced and sang before the golden calf.

I'm crying as I write. Lord, will I ever see my friend again?

Dear Friend,

God has called Moses to another meeting on the mountain. Clouds swirl around Sinai's jagged peak like a holy covering. I wonder how long our leader will be gone this time.

The events of the past few weeks have been frightful for us all, but especially for Saul. I'll be so glad when we can all settle down in a real home again. A five-year-old should not have to wander aimlessly forever.

I had an idea on how to cheer him up. "Hey Saul, follow me. I have a surprise for you."

We hiked across a clearing where last evening's wind drew swirly patterns in the sand. Saul skipped ahead of me, stooping to pick up smooth grayish blue stones along the way. "Come here," I called to him. "I want you to see this."

My brother's eyes widened when he spotted a stack of boulders. Between each rock, narrow spaces served as cozy dens for small desert animals like the rock hyrax. I pointed to a set of paw prints. "It looks like somebody lives here," I whispered.

Saul and I searched for more tracks and talked about our favorite animals. He is not the same little boy whose squeals and endless questions used to drive me nuts. But neither am I the same. God has changed me where it matters most—on the inside. I am more patient now and not as critical of others. I spend more time listening to a person's heart—what they are really saying, instead of what I think they said.

Change is good if it causes us to look into our hearts. As Grandfather used to say, "A life unchanged is a life only half-lived." The farther we travel, the more I understand his words.

Dear Friend,

Grandmother was heating a small pot of water over the fire today.

"What's that for?" Saul asked.

"It's for your Mama. Wait here," said Grandmother, and hurried into the tent.

Mama cried out in a voice I have not heard before. Something is terribly wrong! Saul ran to get Papa, who assured us that everything is fine. Mama is in labor.

"Soon you will be a big brother," said Papa, tousling Saul's hair.

Saul sneaked inside to visit Mama and then burst from the tent like a runaway rabbit, shouting, "We're going to have a baby! We're going to have a baby!"

Word spread from tent to tent about the woman who was about to give birth. With so many now absent from our congregation, the thought of a new life sent excitement rippling throughout the encampment. Mama, who never seeks out attention, would blush if she knew how many people were waiting to hear her baby's first cry.

Papa paced. I felt like I needed to do something to help, but what?

A familiar voice called my name. Tova! She said she'd heard the big news about Mama from a woman who knows the woman who used to know the family next to us. Ha!

"A team of oxen could not have kept me away," joked Tova.

I had so much I wanted to say to her, but my words were choked with emotion. "I thought you … I wondered if your family …"

"Abigail, you don't have to say anything. I understand," said Tova.

Then she told me the best news ever. "God has been patient. I guess he knew that I would come to my senses sooner or later."

She explained how she spent one evening out under the stars. Gazing at the heavens, she asked God to help her to believe— really believe. And he did.

"My parents keep asking what has happened to me." Tova pointed to her heart. "I tell them that God has changed the way I feel inside. It's hard to explain, Abby, but it's as if I don't need to worry anymore."

I hugged her like I would hug a sister. "No need to explain; I know exactly what you mean."

Meanwhile, It's past lunchtime and I'm still waiting for my baby sister to arrive.

Dear Friend,

The desert changed into its nightclothes as the sun dropped lower in the west. Nobody ever told me a baby would take this long to arrive.

"Is everything okay?" I asked Grandmother.

"Everything is fine, just fine," she assured me. "It won't be long now."

"Come on, baby. Hurry!" I kept whispering.

Mama cried out, followed by the high-pitched sound I have been longing to hear for months. "Waaa-aaaa! WAAA-AAAA!"

I wanted to rush into the tent, but Grandmother called, "Not so fast; give us a few more minutes."

When a second baby cried out, pandemonium followed!

TWINS! WE HAVE TWINS!

A little while later, we tiptoed in to see Mama. Grandmother washed both babies and wrapped each snugly in spotless linen cloths.

Papa's eyes glistened with tears as we admired not one but two wrinkly new babies. "Aren't they beautiful?" Mama said weakly.

Papa reached for the baby closest to him. "Meet Jacob," said Mama.

Mama motioned for me to come closer. "And this is Hannah. Her name means 'hope.'"

"Baby Hannah," I whispered, stroking her silky cheek. "I've waited so long to meet you."

Dear Friend,

Well, it looks like my journal is no longer a secret. After the grand arrival of my new brother and sister, I dashed straight over to my bed, slid the journal out of my secret hiding place and wrote as fast as I could. I wanted to get everything down before I lost a single thought. Ben was delighted and keeps threatening to read the entire thing from beginning to end. I would just die! I'll need to think of a new place to hide it from now on.

I'd like to say that we all fell into a deep sleep after the excitement of Hannah and Jacob's birth. Not so! In a few hours it will be dawn. Hungry cries in the night remind us all that our family has grown since the last sunrise.

Dear Friend,

Moses has finally returned from the mountain. After begging God to forgive our sins, God called us stubborn, stiff-necked people, but here's the good news: He did not give up on us nor forsake us.

Since Moses' return, we have built a tabernacle according to God's exact instructions. There the Lord promises to speak to us if we commit to trusting him with all our hearts. Outside the door of the tabernacle stands the pillar—the familiar reminder of God's loving presence.

Word has it that we will continue on our journey soon. In a strange sort of way, I will miss this place. I'll miss the rose finch calling to me at sunrise and the soft-eyed gazelles grazing near the base of the great mountain. I'll even miss the smell of dew-dampened thorn bushes.

Someday I will tell the story of our journey to my children and grandchildren. They'll sigh and ask why I never gave up.

I will point heavenward.

"God would not hear of it," I'll tell them, "for his love would not turn me loose."

Life Issue: **I want make my faith my own.**

Spiritual Building Block: **TRUST**

Do the following activities to increase your trust in God.

Think About It:

As you read this section on trust, jot down your own thoughts on the subject.

Trust is like the wind; we can't see it, but we do see what happens when it rustles the leaves of our favorite tree. Trust is invisible, but powerful.

The Bible has much to say about trust. Trust brings us joy. ("In him our hearts rejoice, for we trust in his holy name." Psalm 33:21 NIV) It helps us to sort through confusion, and make wise choices. ("Trust in the LORD with all your heart and lean not on your own understanding; in all your ways acknowledge him, and he will make your paths straight." Proverbs 3:5–6) Trusting in God also gives us a safe place to run when we are afraid. ("When I am afraid, I will trust in you." Psalm 56:3)

Trust is a conscious choice we all must make. Think of it as a fire drill. Why would anyone wait until their smoke alarm sounds before coming up with a plan of escape? A wise person plans for emergencies in order to react quickly. The same is true in our relationship with God. When stressful times enter our lives, it is natural to react by wanting to run away. If we can outrun a stressful situation, it won't be able to hurt us—or so we think. Can you recall a time when you felt so afraid, you wanted to turn and run? When we plan ahead and make a firm decision to trust God no matter what, he prepares us to face the ups and downs of life.

Friends and loved ones will sometimes disappoint us. (Who hasn't felt the pain of a broken promise, or even worse—a broken relationship?) But when we make a decision to trust God, we have his promise that no matter what life brings our way, he will not desert us. He is worthy of our trust and devotion.

As we invite him to work in our lives, a wonderful thing happens. We find ourselves relaxing more and worrying less. We begin to recognize and celebrate God's fingerprint on everyday situations. When we live a life of trust, it causes others to wonder about our faith, too. When they ask questions, it gives us a chance to share God's love in a personal way.

Believers today marvel at the Israelites' journey through the wilderness. It would have been easy for them to give up, but they made a choice to trust God for direction. When the going got rough, they chose to believe that he would continue providing their daily needs. For thirty years, they moved ahead as God directed, and paused only when he asked them to.

Their experience seems almost impossible, but trusting God made all the difference. How do you think YOU would have fared on such a journey?

Talk About It:

If you could place your level of trust on a scale of 1 to 10, how would it measure up? Does your faith in God shift like the wind, or is it calm and sure—always ready to meet the next challenge?

Talking about trust is different than actually living it. In order to trust someone completely, you must first develop a close relationship. That takes time. Have you set aside a special time each day to get better acquainted with God? Do you talk to him as you would a best friend, or do you call on him only in an emergency?

God created you with a special purpose in mind. Trust him to help you find it, and you will know the key to a life of happiness and satisfaction.

Talk to a close friend or pastor or teacher who you trust about your faith. A great place to begin is to discuss your reaction to this book: Believers today marvel at the Israelites' journey through the wilderness. It would have been easy for them to give up, but they made a choice to trust God for direction. When the going got rough, they chose to believe that he would continue providing their daily needs. For thirty years, they moved ahead as God directed and paused only when he asked them to.

Their experience seems almost impossible, but trusting God made all the difference. How do you think you would have fared on such a journey?

Try It:

Talk to a parent, pastor, or older friend about their Christian journey. Ask for specific examples of how God helped them through a difficult experience. Pray for them as you remember those examples, and thank God for His faithfulness in their lives and yours.

Think about Bible verses that remind you of God's faithfulness and love. Try memorizing a verse a week, either on your own or with a friend or family member. By the end of a year, you'll know fifty-two verses by heart! Trust grows as we bury his word in our hearts.